SAVE THE DATE

CARRIE AARONS

Do you want your **FREE** Carrie Aarons eBook?

All you have to do is **sign up for my newsletter**, and you'll immediately receive your free book!

To the women who believe that, sometimes, a really good pair of shoes is even better than romance.

1

Sometimes I wish I was forewarned, or I guess aware, to soak in the moment right before something pivotal happened.

A Monday morning quarterback kind of feeling, a knowledge that something cosmic was about to go down. Like the day before I got my first period. That song change the minute before I got in my first fender bender.

And the four seconds that lead up to me meeting Reese Collins.

But, I guess that's life. And by life, I mean being whacked, blindsided by an event that you weren't prepared for. I wish I had known, in that moment, the effect this boy was going to have on my life. How much trouble we'd get ourselves into, the deep conversations we'd share. The lasting bond we'd create.

But timing was never on my side when it came to Reese.

We met as awkward, gangly preteens at a backyard barbecue, forced to play together by fathers who had become the best of buddies at their very competitive men's league basketball games. He was into *Star Wars*, video games and baseball. I loved reading, cutting out posters from magazines of that week's latest heartthrob, and playing with my St. Bernard, Waldo.

We couldn't have been more different, and yet, we became the best of friends. Inseparable. Pranksters till the end. A ride or die kind of relationship, the ones where you'd get detention just so the other wouldn't have to do it alone.

But high school ended, and college sprang on us like an alarm clock you keep hitting to turn off. We stayed close; but how close can texting and email, and the monthly phone call, really keep you?

I stayed local, he moved away. Years and other friendships and significant others shoved us that much more apart.

And now, I sit in front of my laptop, an opened email sitting on my browser saying that he was coming to Philadelphia for a job interview, and was I free for dinner?

My mind wanders to the pact, and if he's thought about it as our thirtieth birthdays neared. Two weeks and five days apart, we used to give each other birthday punches on the arm until our extremities were numb.

The deal we made when we were fifteen is flashing through my mind as I sit in my apartment, sirens screaming through Center City ten stories below me. My hands hesitate over the keys, because I don't know how to respond.

I twirl a long strand of corn silk blond, a color I completely overpay for but still looks natural, through my fingers and chew my full bottom lip. What is it that my mom always calls my mouth? A cupid's bow, because of my smaller, curved upper lip.

The skin above my mouth is hard and crusted over with a face mask I should have washed off twenty minutes ago, but was too lazy to get up and do so. I was pretty okay looking, could even be beautiful if I got the highlighter on my cheekbones just right and my hair wasn't full of dry shampoo. But the wrinkle lines had started to mark my face as my twenties neared their end. Yet, I still got a pimple somewhere on my face weekly. What was with that? I wish my body would pick; young or old. I didn't want to be bothered by both ends of the spectrum.

And then I got caught up in my Facebook feed, looking at cute dogs and babies of people I hadn't spoken to in over a decade. Priorities, am I right?

"What the hell am I doing?" I mentally smack myself, because of course I'm going to get dinner with Reese when he's in town.

Laying my fingers, the nails of which are grown out with light pink polish and really need a fresh manicure, on the keyboard, I type an email back to my best friend.

> *Reese,*
>
> *Of course I can grab dinner, but I don't want to hear any bragging about how amazing your interview goes. Because we both know you'll charm the healers of little people, and will end up charming this city away from me.*
>
> *You're buying though, since the medical field definitely pays better than a dying newspaper.*
>
> *I'm only meeting if you bring me one of those muffins from that bakery on that street I like.*
>
> *Tolerate you,*
>
> *Erin*
>
> *P.S.- Actually can't wait, get ready for picklebacks.*

The email was full of inside jokes, and I close my laptop smiling. I've become too cynical lately, which means it's probably been too long since we've seen each other. Reese and I are like opposite sides of a battery, we charge the other to be fun and eccentric. Although, Reese was usually the one who did this better than I did.

It had been three months since I'd visited him in Dallas,

since we'd gorged on breakfast foods at that tiny bakery near his apartment and I'd confessed my undying love to muffins. And I wasn't lying when I said he was taking me to dinner, my position as Editorial Director at the city's biggest newspaper, The Philadelphia Journal, had more prestige in the title than it did in the paycheck.

Standing from my suede gray couch, my Christmas present to myself when I found it on clearance at Pottery Barn, I walk across my modest apartment. It wasn't the shoebox I'd rented when I first moved into Philadelphia from the suburbs of Pennsylvania. And it didn't have three roommates that came along with it; no, I'd promised myself that I'd spring for solitude even if it cut into my budget a little more than shacking up with a girlfriend.

I was almost thirty, after all.

And then the pact pops back into my brain, and my palms begin to sweat. Because what if Reese remembered too, and was coming back to collect on promises past?

Oh, shit on a shingle. I wasn't ready to say "I do." Especially to the boy who used to put worms in my hair.

The heated exhaust from a SEPTA bus hits me square in the face, and damn does it feel good, and smell horrible, to be back on my East Coast.

It's been too long, and I even smiled when the Uber driver, who dropped me off in the middle of the city from the airport, had slammed on his horn and flipped the bird at a tailgating car. Dallas, the current location where I worked and played, was great ... but there was just something about the bluntness of Philly and its inhabitants that I craved. The south was amiable, slower, and everyone was pleasant. Being from the suburbs of Pennsylvania, a stone's throw from the city of brotherly love, I grew up in the chaos, harsh language, and cold.

Crossing the street at a crosswalk, I add not having to pay for a car as a plus for taking the job here. The Children's Hospital of Philadelphia looms over me as the humidity settles into every crevice of my suit, and I square my shoulders. It's hot as hell, but I'd be an idiot not to don a crisp tie and jacket for this interview. CHOP is big time, especially to a NICU nurse, which is what I've worked as for the last eight years. This is the whale of jobs in my field, and I wanted to slay it like I was Moby Dick.

I check in at the security desk, telling the guard I'm here for an interview.

"Which floor?" she asks, not even looking up at me.

I turn on the charm, making sure my dimple does an extra flex when Dorothy, I spot her name tag, looks up. "The NICU, hoping to become a part of the team."

That gets a smile in my direction, and not like it matters what the guards think of me, but I see it as a positive on my scorecard of this interview day.

Dorothy tells me to wait in the lobby, and Joann Callens, the President of Human Resources, will be down shortly.

I walk to the bathroom, wanting to wipe the sweat from my neck and wash my hands before Joann comes down. I consider myself in the mirror after I pee and splash water on my face. The same light green eyes and dark brown, almost black, hair that have always met me stare back, but I can tell I look tired. Partly from the flight, and partly because of the argument I got in to right before boarding it.

Was I insane for considering a move back home, essentially, and leaving my entire life behind?

To be honest, the move couldn't come at a better time. The hospital I currently worked at was about to go under, despite all we'd done to work our asses off to save it. They were going to go corporate, and we all knew what happened when those vultures came in and picked apart the bones of a hospital and it's staff.

Life in Dallas was becoming monotonous, and as an East Coast native, I missed snow. I'm sure I wouldn't miss it after I had to walk through two feet of snow to work after the first storm, but seasons would be nice. And to stop having to walk funny seven months out of the year due to my balls being so fucking sweaty.

But most of all, things with Renée were ... complicated.

After two years of dating on and off, she wanted a ring. And even though she made me happy and I think I love her, there was something holding me back. Maybe it was the way she tried to hand hold me into doing what she wanted. Or the fact that she couldn't stand to watch even one minute of the Phillies on TV, even though I sat through hours of her reality TV trash.

But it wasn't just stupid little things like that ... when I looked at her, I just didn't see my future wife. It was a horrible thing to say about someone who was supposed to be, and had been, your person for a long time ... but there it was.

We were on a break, our fifth this year and it was only June. That was saying something. She was pissed I was taking an interview so far away, that I could just up and leave without considering her and our relationship. But I was considering it, just not the outcome she wanted.

I'm only waiting five minutes in the lobby when Joann comes down.

"Reese, great to meet you. I'm Joann Callens." An older looking woman fiercely struts toward me, and you can tell she means business. The pantsuit, the hospital badge hanging from her neck, the perfectly flattened bob haircut.

But the smile on her face is endearing, and it's the one thing that keeps me from second-guessing my chances here. This woman knows her power, how to wield it, you can just sense it about her. But hopefully, and it seems so, Joann Callens is fair enough to consider all angles of my personality and work.

"Thank you for the opportunity to interview for the position." I shake her outstretched hand, trying to match the strong grip she gives back.

"Hope you had a good flight, you're from here, correct?"

I nod, smiling. "Grew up just outside the city. Lifelong Jim's fan, so if you tell me you like Pat's or Gino's, I may have to reconsider my application here."

A Philadelphians choice of cheesesteak joint said a lot about them.

Joann hesitates a beat, and then grins. "I like Jim's too, so I think we're off to a good start."

She walks me around the hospital a bit, pointing out floors and rooms, waving to staff, detailing the mission of CHOP. I try not to let my mouth hang open at the top-of-the-line technology they're sporting. The hospital I work at now is good, but this place puts it to shame.

We finally reach our destination, the stereotypical conference room made of glass that overlooks a courtyard on the side of the hospital. I often wonder about these courtyards, and why hospitals put them in. I think the architects or people who don't work in the medical field think they'll be utilized for a peaceful outdoor space for families of patients, or for the staff on their breaks. I bite my tongue to keep from smirking, because no one ever uses them. They're too preoccupied with what is going on inside the hospital walls, whether it's concerning family members or patients.

Joann starts off with all of the regular questions: tell me about your career thus far, what are your strengths, weaknesses, what would you do in this situation, etc.

And then she asks me why I got into the field, the one question that I always know has an underlying meaning for a male nurse candidate. Whether it should or not.

"Well, I know you can't ask me this in an interview, but you're probably wondering why a male would want to become a nurse. Much less a nurse in neonatal intensive care." I incline my head at her, knowing that most people are shocked to find a man in this line of work. "First off, I am a nurse because I love working with patients on a more intimate level than a doctor's work allows. I enjoy getting to know their quirks and personalities, holding their hands when they get a needle or joking with them when they're finally allowed to eat a meal after surgery."

I watch Joann lean forward, and I know she's hanging on my every word. It's not insincere either, I really do feel that way. I love my job. But, I'm also an expert salesman when it comes to myself, especially when I'm trying to get in on something I really desire.

I go on. "I love what I do. I'm committed, I'm passionate, and I will do everything possible to make my patients feel comfortable, even if they are two-day-old newborns. I think there is a delicate balance when working in the NICU, because you really have two patients, even though you're charged with caring for one. Parents are your other priority, and I thrive when I need to help these parents, who are both grieving and overjoyed, bond with their little one in the most normal way that we can allow given their current medical situation."

After I'm done with my little diatribe, she doesn't break eye contact with me, just leans back and assesses me, a light smirk on her face. And I know I've nailed it. I'm not cocky, just confident. There are a few things I excel at in life, and I know what those are. Nursing, and being able to hold a conversation, are two of them.

My mother's voice comes into my head just then, *"Never doubt the things you know you are good at. There is enough to feel self-conscious about, don't let it be your strengths."*

Never having had a daughter, I think she built me up too much as a little boy with the self-esteem talks. But I can't say they didn't work.

After another five minutes of small talk Joann stood, extending her hand for me to shake. "We'll be in touch. Thanks for coming in, Reese."

As I left CHOP, I shook off the interview nerves. My body relaxed, and was in sudden desperate need of a beer.

And then I thought of Erin. And the pact. And if she'd thought of it at all since I told her I'd be coming to town.

The sun is setting over the city, making the metallic windows of the buildings gleam off of each other, as I wrench open the door to the seafood restaurant I made a reservation at.

"Nice to see that your running late hasn't changed a bit, Carter." I almost run smack dab into Reese, who is waiting for me in the lobby.

I hold my hands up, panting. "Sorry, sorry, last minute edit to tomorrow's paper and I had to do some creative rearranging. And don't call me by my last name, you know I hate that."

I push my knotted hair out of my face and suck in a breath, a side-effect of running when I hadn't exercised in who knew how long. I was slacking on my workouts, yet my gym membership was still coming out of my bank account each month. Something needed to be done about that.

It's only then do I really take in my best friend. Every time I see Reese as a grown man, it somehow continues to shock me. When I'm not with him, I think of him in childhood terms, the way he looked when we used to hunt for guppies out by the creak or his appearance as fireflies blinked around his face on a summer night.

Seeing him as a man ... I'm always a little unnerved at how attractive he is. I guess he was always cute, with that boyish charm, the dimple, the perfectly unruly brown hair cropped close on the sides. But as he's aged, that thing that happens to men began to happen to Reese. He looks more rugged, his shoulders filled out and muscles have replaced the gangly boy I once knew. Dark stubble dotted his jaw and cheeks, and his eyes became even more impossible to stare at ... the way the brown mixed with the light green was hard to pull your eyes away from. Reese had always been taller, but now he towered over me, a good foot above where I stood.

I'm a woman, and I can only deny it to myself so much when I see a hot guy. Which is why it's hard now to associate my best friend Reese with the gorgeous specimen who stands before me.

"I thought you were going to blow me off. Kind of like junior prom." His dimple pops out, and that paired with the suit does strange things to my stomach.

I can't help but frown. Maybe I'm just in my head about the pact. *Stop being a weirdo*, I scold myself.

Reese motions to the hostess that we're ready, and I follow him to our table. "You're never going to let me live that down, huh? I had a chance to kiss Mike Hull under the bleachers, what other choice did I have?"

I'd ditched my best friend for the dance we were supposed to share on prom night to make out with a guy who now worked as a used car salesman in our hometown. Looking back, I had been an idiot.

Although, most of my choices in men up until now have been idiotic.

"You had the choice to dance with me to Boyz II Men, that's what you had. Good to see you, peas."

We had decided, after we'd watched *Forest Gump* for the first time, that I would be peas and Reese would be carrots. It was a kid's rationale that led to this decision. I was shorter, and Reese had reasoned that I had boobs (barely), therefore, he was the carrot.

He scoops me up into a hug before we sit down, and I can't help but hold on a little longer. I forgot for a while how much I missed him, how big a part in my life he played.

The restaurant is packed on a Thursday night, people ready for the weekend. It's low lighting, modern, industrial feel and blue accents are designed to make the diner feel as if they're eating in an old fish market. Or so I read from our food columnist in one of the Sunday editions.

Reese stares at me, studying my face when we're seated across from each other. I pick up the menu, my stomach grumbling.

"You look good, kid." He cocks his head to the side. "A little tired, but good."

"Is that your way of telling me I look like crap, but only a little crap? I'm getting the surf and turf by the way, because my benefactor can afford it." I snap my menu shut.

The waitress comes and we order wine and put in our meals.

"What, no picklebacks?" Reese smiles, shrugging out of his suit jacket and hanging it on the back of his chair.

"It's early, yet, carrots." I smirk, up for some rounds at the bar after. It's been a hell of a week. "Now tell me about your interview."

We eat lazily, recounting old stories and drinking a little, okay *a lot*, of wine. Reese tells me that he knocked his interview out of the park, and I tell him how terrible the paper is. I wish I knew what it was like to love my job. Well ... I sort of did, but my passion was more of a free time hobby right now than it was an actual career.

The way Reese talks about being a neonatal nurse inspires dreams. He speaks about it as if he slays dragons or something, like it's all consuming and he gets up every day, completely happy and content in his position.

I forgot how he could light me up like a lightbulb, how he could make everything around him shine.

"God, do you ever look at pictures of yourself from high school and think, I was so much skinnier then? I will never be that skinny again." I sulk into my glass of red, well and drunk by this point.

Reese raises an eyebrow at me. "Yeah, guys don't really do that. I do look back at those pictures and think, 'Why in the hell did I cut my hair like that?'"

"Lord, that crew cut was awful. And you'd do that horrible spike in the front thing with that gel stick ... you looked like a boy band member." I giggle.

"You thought it was cute. Or, at least, Mary Kate Smith did." He winks, a dirty secret of the past from when he got to third base with her in my living room.

"You're disgusting. I had to scrub those couch cushions before my parents got home, because I thought they would smell like sex. Morgan always kept going on about how our parents could tell if any kissing or tomfoolery had gone on. Probably so I wouldn't do any of it." I laughed, remembering.

"Tomfoolery, eh? So you weren't a prude, you were just petrified of your parents finding out." His glass meets his lips, and I find myself watching the action.

I shrug, the liquor invading my brain. "Who said I was a prude? You just weren't around when I got my rocks off. I didn't kiss and tell."

Reese's hazel eyes shimmer green with the greed to know more details. But he doesn't ask. "Well, for what it's worth, I like how you look now. More curves, instead of those skinny little chicken legs and bony hips you used to have."

I throw my napkin at him. "Jerk. I didn't even bring up the puka shell necklace you used to wear, but now I will. You've never even surfed in your life, yet you had that stupid 2000s version of a choker necklace on at all times."

Reese laughs, a booming, jubilant sound escaping from his lips. I haven't seen him in months, and somehow forgot how lethal that boyish little dimple that marks his right cheek is. He may look like a man now, but when he laughs, I'm transported back in time to the days when we used to play under the willow tree in his backyard.

I need to remind myself of his monster of a girlfriend, because my thoughts are going sideways and I'm being a creep.

"So, how's Renée? Of Reese and Renée, of course." I smirk, because I can't help but be a bitch.

Renée was Reese's girlfriend, or so I thought they were still together. She was a buyer for Macy's out of Dallas, had naturally pin-straight auburn hair that hung to the middle of her back, and could put Carrie Underwood's legs to shame. No, I wasn't jealous whatsoever. Cue eye roll.

His boo, who he'd been seeing on and off for two years, had an Instagram similar to my own, with less followers. Somehow, that fact always made me smile.

Oh, and did I mention she also hated me? Yeah, for some reason, the female best friend of her boyfriend, who he confided in more than her, wasn't at the top of her bestie list. Go figure.

Not that I minded, because I wasn't her biggest fan either. They were too perfect, the sheen coming off of their relationship sweet as sugar. Which meant that, of course, it was all bullshit. Reese had told me how sour the pairing was on the inside, how she nagged him, how he hated it. Yet, my best friend stuck with her, because he loved her. Or so he said.

I think he stayed because, well ... Reese always stayed. He was somewhat of a girlfriend slut. Meaning, he was always in a relationship. He was the kind of male who had no idea how to function outside of one, he needed a woman to tell him which way was up.

To someone like me, who was fiercely independent, it just made no sense. I would run for the hills if anyone tried to tell me squat, much less control my daily narrative. I never understood how he could care so little about being codependent.

"I wouldn't know, I haven't spoken to her since I landed." His eyes don't leave mine when he takes another sip.

And once more, the promise we swore to uphold tickles the front of my brain.

Picklebacks are worse than I remember.

It started as a joke when we were in college, to find the grossest shot we could muster drinking. We'd vowed to visit each other every month, her at Villanova and me at Drexel. We'd always met at some restaurant or café, and then when we turned twenty-one, a bar. On a particularly bad night for Erin, the latest moron had broken her heart, she told me she wanted to get fall-down drunk. And of course, I'd obliged.

After about six rounds, we just started doing stupid shit for fun. Drinking games, truth or dare, and then, find the grossest shot.

The bartender had poured us picklebacks, and I'd almost puked mine up on the wooden bar top. It had been our thing ever since.

I watch as Erin tips it back, her long throat quivering as the liquid slides down it. Her blond hair, the color of sunflower petals, is longer than I remember, with short bangs framing her face. She's lost weight since the last time I saw her, but those curves are still there. They have been since senior year of high school, when I could no longer ignore the roundness of my best friend's breasts or tone of her ass. I can't say I haven't thought about her in a bikini, or the one time I caught her naked in my childhood bedroom. To be honest, that was shameful spank bank go-to for years.

It might still be.

Erin's long legs are crossed, the skirt she wore to work hiked up and two buttons on the white collared-shirt undone to reveal the smattering of freckles on her chest. She looked hot, in a girl-next-door kind of way, which had always been her signature.

"So, you know what's coming up, right?" I broach the subject, because of course thirty doesn't just mean reaching an age milestone for the two of us.

And of course, because I've had too much to drink and ever since I got the call about the position at CHOP, I've been thinking about Erin and our marriage pact.

She winces from the aftertaste of the shot, but lays an unsteady grip on my forearm. "Oh, shut up. We're not talking about this."

Deadpan, I look at her. "We promised that when we turned thirty, if we weren't married to other people, then we'd get married to each other."

It's true. We'd taken the oath in my backyard under the willow tree after Erin's first boyfriend, Dan the football jerk as we referred to him, had dumped her. Pinky promise, spit on the hands and everything.

Erin laughs, but the humor doesn't reach her eyes. "We made that pact when we were fifteen! Get the fuck out of here!"

I level with her, spinning out on the idea as if a lightbulb has gone on and it's the most genius thing we could ever do.

"Come on, think about it! There would be no lies or false bullshit. We'd shoot straight with each other. It would be fun, like having a sleepover with your best friend every night! And we're both hot, the sex would be good."

Not for the first time, my blood heats thinking about what it would be like to have Erin on top of me.

"Yuck, stop it now. You're going to make me barf up that pickleback." Erin shudders as if I've just told her the most disgusting joke in the world.

I brush it off, a little hurt, with a sarcastic barb. "Fine, but don't come crying to me when you turn into an old maid."

Erin rubs her ankle, the back of her shoe slipping off her heel. "Technically, by nineteenth century standards, I'm already an old maid. But, Elizabeth Bennett finally found her prince in the end. And she didn't have dating apps or sex toys. So ... I think I'm doing slightly better than her."

This is how she's always been. Sarcastic. Smart. Independent. Gorgeous. And somewhat detached.

It's become worse, the ice-cold heart, since her parents announced their divorce a couple years ago. It had been messy and mean, and I could see how it slowly destroyed the small hope Erin had ever had in the emotion of love.

She had never been the most affectionate person. In fact, most people we grew up with knew she was like a diamond. Shiny, attractive, someone everyone was drawn to. But Erin was cold, off limits to a lot of people, could be cutting. Except to me. I knew how to get under that rock-hard exterior.

"Ah, so a rich, semi-aloof land owner who likes art and long walks through the woods is going to come along and sweep you off your feet?"

"I can't believe you remember the plot of *Pride & Prejudice*." Erin laughs, a strong, rich sound that always came from the back of her throat.

I'd forgotten how that throaty voice affected me, a smoker's tone coming from such a thin, petite woman. If you ever spoke to her on the phone, you might envision a burly truck driver. I'm not sure why it made her more attractive, but it always had.

I'd also forgotten how to hide the crush I had on my best friend. After eighteen years, you'd think I'd be an expert at putting on the front, but it seemed that I'd gotten rusty with the time and distance.

"I'm the bookish one between us, remember? The nerd, as you used to call me. And just because it's a romance doesn't mean I didn't read every book assigned to us in high school. And then there is the fact that you made me watch the movie with Kiera Knightly about a million times."

My beer is almost empty, and I motion to the bartender to bring another. We've drank way too much, and she has to work tomorrow and I have a plane to catch, but neither of us seems to care. It's been too long since we did this.

"So? I love the movie, whatever." She shrugs, annoyed that I pointed out a soft spot in her armor.

"Back to the pact ..." I half-tease.

I can't say I haven't thought about what a marriage with Erin would look like. What it would feel like if we actually stepped over the cliff. What her lips would feel like if I kissed them.

"What, is Renée holding out on you? Are you really that horny that you'd resort to me?" Erin scoffs, leaning back on her bar stool a little.

She keeps bringing up Renée, and something tells me it's a defense mechanism.

"You're never a last resort, Erin. I thought I taught you that." My voice is serious now. "You know you've been the top woman in my life."

I wasn't joking when I said that. Anytime one of my girlfriends gave me an ultimatum, or asked me to distance myself from my best friend, I'd chosen her. I'd tried, every time she broke up with one of those boneheads she dated, to remind her that she deserved the very best kind of man to love her.

She salutes me and giggles. "Yes, sir."

I lean forward, the alcohol and my thoughts possessing me.

Erin's eyes grow wide with panic. "What are you doing, Reese?"

"Just sit still, peas." I palm her cheek.

I probably shouldn't do this, have come close a couple of times but never acted on it. But now, with the pact and our thirtieth birthdays looming over our heads, I want to know what it would be like. I want her to stop laughing about us together. I'm genuinely curious.

I'm not sure why Erin lets me move my mouth closer to hers, and it suddenly strikes me that I'm doing this with liquid courage in both of our systems. I shouldn't taste her this way, our first, if only, kiss should be sober. But I can't stop now, not when she's allowing me to get this close.

Shutting my brain off, I close the gap between us, touching my mouth to hers. Years of friendship, hinge on this small, but oh so big, action.

She's salty, from the shot, and I push my lips against her cupid's bow mouth, inhaling the citrus of her perfume.

I've kissed probably a hundred women, which is why Erin called me a manwhore sometimes, but none of them had been like this.

The velvet of her cheek is smooth under my fingers, and I can feel the muscles in her jaw work as we kiss. Our mouths explore for a few seconds, friction sparking between our lips, before I slip my tongue past her teeth. The minute it touches hers, something in my chest loosens, like the exact key to the lock on my heart has finally been found and turned.

Erin breaks off first, suddenly, coughing and giggling loudly as she reaches for her martini and taking a giant gulp, finishing the drink.

A nervous laugh leaves the lips I was just kissing. "All right, carrots, you got your shot. And I think it proved that we're not meant to live happily ever after."

I have to swallow my disbelief, keep it from clouding my features. Because if anything, that kiss proved to me that everything I'd been looking for in a woman had been sitting right in front of my eyes for eighteen years.

And now I'm going to have to go back to pretending that we're just friends, because she clearly didn't feel any of that.

5

ERIN

I've never been an overly emotional person. In fact, at one point, I questioned if I even had them.

Yeah, I love my sister, Morgan, and my parents. I have friends, good ones even, and I've always had Reese. But ... the way other people outwardly act toward each other, I've just never been able to connect with that. Hugging, braiding each other's hair, freaking out when a boy texts and they all decide what to respond with as a group.

Needing to go to the bathroom in giggling hordes. I never understood that one. Who needed a buddy system to pee in a public restroom?

Don't get me wrong, that doesn't mean I'm absolutely not girly. I love all things clothes, bags, candles, flower arrangements and shoes. *Especially* shoes. It's why I started my blog two years ago, Shoes and the City.

The blog that almost every single one of my coworkers has no idea about, even if I do have over two hundred thousand followers on Instagram. And even if I do spend every single waking moment, when I'm not work, curating content in the hopes of making it my full-time career.

As of now, I feel like I'm living a double life. The shit I comb through by day at my corporate, boring job. And the passion that lights me up on nights and weekends. Jesus, it basically sounds like my blog is my mistress.

But still, despite all of that not needing to gossip and giggle, I feel the need to download on someone about that kiss with Reese.

After he'd cupped my face and tasted me, my head swimming from the situation and alcohol, we'd laughed it off awkwardly. Then we'd finished our drinks while talking about the latest episode of *Game of Thrones*, and had said goodbye outside of our respective Ubers.

I'd texted him this morning to have a safe flight, and he'd sent back a thumbs-up, but I couldn't help but feel like something had changed last night. Reese wasn't even in Philadelphia anymore, and yet I felt his presence everywhere.

I open Photoshop, ready to lose myself in editing photos of my favorite summer sandals that I'd snapped over the weekend. But as I flip through the pictures, trying to pick the best, I find myself studying the same one for fifteen minutes. Kind of like when your mind is elsewhere and you read the same sentence in a book eight times.

That kiss was going to hang over us forever now. We'd managed to tamp down any flirtations or close calls for eighteen years. We'd gotten through puberty and our drunken college days without slipping up. And now, why now?

I'll tell you why. Because Reese had to go on and bring up that dumb pinky promise, and it was putting pressure on us.

Worse ... I had liked the kiss. That was weird, it felt wrong. He was like my brother. He was my best friend.

But it had felt so right. I half-hated that it did. But the other half of me was so confused that I wanted to try again. And now he was back in Dallas with his sort-of girlfriend, and the fact that I was sour about that confused me even more.

Overall, I was just very fucking confused.

I lose myself in editing for a while, checking my Instagram to make sure the photos and blog posts I was preparing really matched the overall theme of my brand, and went through my email. I'd been at this blogging game for two years, and was only just now, in the past six months or so, being approached about deals with companies to represent products or post advertisements.

I'd sunk my own money and time into the clothes, shoes, makeup, photo shoots and more over a year and a half to make my blog relevant and trending. It was honestly pretty fucking cool that all of my hard work was now being rewarded, and if it kept up, this could sustain me as a full-time career. I was already making more on my blogging than my shitty paycheck from The Journal, and as I read through my email, two new clothing companies wanted to partner with me.

My brain could only be distracted for so long, and soon I was on Facebook, typing in Reese's name after stalking on my timeline for a bit. I clearly had a problem, as did the rest of the world, with my social media addiction.

His page popped up, and I immediately clicked over to his photos section, to see if there were any recent pictures of Renée. Part of me wanted to see him making out with her in a nightclub or something, just so I would know that that kiss meant nothing and he was back with his girlfriend of the moment.

But, alas, no such pictures. Which only made my thoughts stew more.

My phone rang and I jumped, alone in my apartment, wondering if Reese had been reading my mind.

But it was only Morgan, my sister, calling for the fifth time this week. She lived twenty minutes from me, and yet we talked each day as if we didn't see each other twice, or sometimes three, times a week.

"My feet look like sausage patties. And my ankles, lord, they don't even exist anymore. Can you remind me that I'll look fabulous someday after this?" Morgan whines into my ear, not even bothering to say hi.

My older sister, by two and a half years, was six months pregnant and not enjoying one single second. She and her husband, Jeff, had finally made the decision to have a baby after six years of marriage. And while I knew she was going to be one awesome mom, she was having a hell of a pregnancy. Terrible morning sickness, back pain, and now she'd started peeing herself whenever she sneezed. It sounded like the best kind of birth control to me.

"After you have the baby, you can come to Pilates and barre with me until you look like Jillian Michaels. Don't worry, I'll tell you when you need to lose the weight."

And I would, because we had the kind of relationship that was brutally honest. We'd always been close, never had that kind of sister rivalry that separated some siblings. But after our parent's divorce five years ago, we'd made a pact to never let anything get between us. And with that, came brutal honesty. If I was being too much of an asshole, or she was whining too much, we let the other know.

"Thanks, Er. Did you get my picture of that unicorn blanket, though? So freaking cute!" This was the fun part of her having a baby girl. The clothes and decor.

I was excited to be an aunt, as long as I could give the little squirt back when she started crying. "Adorable. I was in this secondhand shop the other day and found the cutest little dress from the seventies. It has fringe and is this mustard yellow color. I wanted to die it was so cute. Of course I bought it."

I think I'd spent about a million dollars on this baby already.

But I couldn't help myself. Every time I saw something girly, I picked it up and stored it away for her.

"You're insane. This girl is going to be so well-dressed. Maybe she'll even start a rival blog. Baby Shoes in the Bassinet. Or oh! How about Rock-a-Bye Birkin?" Morgan laughed, cracking herself up.

"And this is why you're not my marketing officer. Leave it to the wannabe-Instagram celebrities like me, okay?" I was nothing if not self-deprecating.

"Fine. How was Reese's Pieces?" Morgan used her nickname for my best friend.

A sour feeling moved down my spine. I got that sick churning in my stomach, like when you get nervous and have to poop. Was I going to feel this way anytime I thought about Reese now? What a stupid thing we did. Why had I let him?

"He was good. Went to dinner after his interview." I kept it short and simple.

And Morgan saw right fucking through me.

"Why are you being weird?" She sounds distracted, like she's walking around their brownstone on the Main Line cleaning.

She probably is, anxious and annoyed that the doctor told her to take it easy. Jeff was a computer engineer, high up in a Fortune 500 company and the sole earner between the two of them. Morgan never needed to work a day in her life if she didn't want to, could just putz around the swanky townhouse they'd bought in the wealthy part of Philly. But, she loved her job as an accountant, and planned to go back after having my niece.

"I'm not being weird." The pitch of my tone was too high. *Fuck.*

"You are *so* being weird. Oh, Erin, did you buy another pair of shoes you can't afford? Don't tell me I have to return another pair of Manolo's because you're too embarrassed ..."

"That was one time!" I cried, annoyed at her.

I'd gone on a drunken shopping spree once after a boozy brunch, maxing out my credit card at Nordstrom. And I'd been so embarrassed the day after, I made Morgan go take six of the pairs back. Yes, six ... whatever, retail therapy made me feel better. Especially after three Bloody Mary's.

"Shit, I have to pee again. Hold that weirdness, we are going to talk about this. I love you, bye!"

And with that, she hung up on me, not even bothering to hear me bid her farewell. That's how we were, the two of us. Sisters. Push and pull, fight and love, able to read the other's mood and thoughts.

For not the first time in my life, I cursed my sister's ability to read me. Because it meant that, eventually, we were going to have to talk about that kiss.

And I still wasn't even sure how I felt about it.

6

REESE

"Hi, Mom," I say as soon as she picks up the phone for our weekly Monday night call.

She and Dad still live in the town I grew up in. Just twenty-five minutes outside of the city, Chester sat right on the Delaware River. It was an ideal place to grow up, and I grew homesick just hearing their voices. Thankfully, I'd be back there soon.

After hearing from Joann just a week after my interview, I needed to make the decision about whether I was going to take the job she'd offered me.

A prestige position in the country's leading NICU, I could further my career and learn techniques and medical procedures that I'd only dreamed about. This was the job to end all job searches. But ... I liked my life here. I really liked Dallas.

And then there was the matter of Renée. Who I'd yet to have a real conversation with about my move, even as I packed one of the last boxes in my apartment to ship to Philadelphia.

You know, because I'd decided I was moving back home and taking the job.

"*Chris*! Come down here, Reese is on the phone!" Mom

screams into the receiver, trying to get my dad in the same room as her so they can both be on speaker phone.

"So, I got the job at CHOP." I can't wait to tell them. I never was any good at suspense or surprises.

"Yeehaw, partner! I'm so happy for you, bud." Mom's voice rings through my phone.

Ever since I moved to Dallas, she thinks I live in some kind of honky-tonk Western movie. I've tried to tell her multiple times that Dallas is just like Philadelphia, just a little warmer with more accents and country music. But essentially, a city is a city no matter how you look at it.

She still doesn't get it though, and will speak to me with a bad Dolly Parton impression on our weekly phone calls. I'm nothing if not a mama's boy, and talking to my parents every Monday night has become a ritual. I've been in Dallas for almost three and a half years, and while I think it was essential for me to move away from home, the job at CHOP is my chance to go back to my roots.

"Oh, I'm so happy I'll have you home! And think of how excited Erin will be! She was over here last week, after visiting Barbara. She is so gorgeous, you know?"

Of course she mentioned Erin straight off. It wasn't obvious or anything that my mom had always wanted my childhood best friend and I to end up together. For years, she'd been telling me that we were just biding our time as friends until life constructed the perfect moment.

Maybe she was right after all. Not that I was going to tell her what had happened when I'd come for the interview.

"How is Barbara doing?" I avoid the Erin subject altogether.

We'd texted on and off the past month that I had been back in Dallas, never once bringing up the kiss. So yeah, we were *really* mature adults.

Mom sighs into the phone. "It's been almost five years,

honey, and still she is so broken up about it. How can you do that to the partner you swore to spend your life with? How do you just fall out of love with someone? I just don't understand."

Barbara and David Carter had been the picture-perfect idea of marriage when I was growing up. Unlike my parents, who clearly loved each other but enjoyed bickering, they held hands all the time, sang songs by the piano at Christmas, and kissed each other in the driveway before they left for work. I'd admired them my entire childhood, and had been jealous of Erin's seemingly perfect family.

It had always been a point of pride for the two of us, how intact our families were. How long our parents had been married. And then, hers fell apart.

One day, shortly after Erin's twenty-fifth birthday, David came home and told Barbara that he didn't love her anymore, and that he wanted a divorce. At the time, I'd been living in New York City, and I'd come home after receiving a call from Erin. It was only the second time in our entire friendship that I'd heard her cry, the first being when she'd broken her arm in tenth grade. And as I drove, the phone on speaker, it was more like hyperventilating than crying coming through the other end, my best friend having a complete meltdown.

I remember holding her, falling asleep on the couch in her childhood basement as her tears dried on her cheeks. I think that was the moment it all changed. The moment where my feelings for her hit me like a full-on tidal wave.

Sure, they'd been quietly brewing in the back of my heart and mind for years. I'd had the schoolboy crush, and then the jealousy. I thought of her while I was away at college, and there were those two times that we'd taken it too far and then never addressed it.

But in that basement, my entire world shifted. I'd held her, her soft breath fanning out on the damp part of my shirt she'd just sobbed into, and I just knew. Knew that someday, maybe not then, but some day, I would be the one to protect her from the worst times. I'd be the one to hold her in the best of times. I felt it so fiercely in that moment that it scared the shit out of me.

And I ran. I moved to Dallas a year later after scouring the country for a job that would take me away. That would keep me from fucking up the only good relationship with a woman I had ever had in my life.

But now I was coming back. And I could sense the shift in the air.

"I don't understand either, but I'm just glad I'm moving home so I can be close to you all again. I miss cheesesteaks and the Phillies."

"We'll have to get tickets to a game this summer, just you, me and your father, like old times." I could hear Mom clap her hands.

I chuckled, remembering our last baseball game. Mom had wanted food in each inning, just like a ten-year-old, and Dad had gotten annoyed that she was interrupting his box score following. She'd even gotten mustard on his notebook, and he was so surly that I'd gotten two extra beers just to get through innings seven through nine.

That was my family though, and I wouldn't trade them for anything.

"All right, honey, you get to packing so I can see you so soon. I have to take the casserole out of the oven. Dust off those boots, ya hear?" Mom laughed at her own bad southern joke.

I rolled my eyes. "Be home soon."

The GrubHub delivery person buzzed up to my apartment, and I got so excited about the Chinese food about to be in my belly that I did a little dance to the door.

As I swung it open, forgetting about the new clarifying mask I was trying for a blog post, the twenty-something kid gave me a look like my hair was on fire or something.

I reached up, touching my cheek, trying to explain. "Whoops. Hazards of the job. Thanks!"

Suddenly famished and a lot embarrassed, I hold out a ten-dollar bill that he grabs in exchange for my bag of food. I see him peer inside, probably thinking that there has to be more people here. But nope, just me. Eating too many containers of various Chinese food that would be enough to feed a small gathering.

After he's gone, I set my spread up on the coffee table, un-pause *Diners, Drive-ins and Dives*, my latest guilty pleasure watch, and sit cross-legged on the floor. Yes, I have a kitchen table, but what single person actually uses one of those? I'm usually eating on the floor or on the couch, in front of the TV, or in my bed before nodding off.

Just as I'm about to shove the first chopstick full of lo mein into my face, my cell buzzes with an incoming call.

One of the only girlfriends I have, Jillian's name lights up the screen and I groan. It's a Saturday night. She's probably out somewhere in the city, just starting her night, and wants me to come out. How do I know this? Because she does this every Saturday night. And every Saturday night, I typically decline.

For being a lifestyle blogger, I don't have much of a lifestyle. Unless you count testing beauty products on date night while eating fried food in my granny-panties. But seriously, I never go out anymore. If I drink more than two glasses of wine, I get a massive hangover in the morning. I could no longer put up with small talk or bad pickup lines.

Welcome to almost thirty.

I pick up the call anyway. "Hey, Jill."

The background noise of a bar infiltrates the speaker in my ear, and I cringe at the loud sounds. "Erin! Come meet me, I'm at Jive!"

"I'm in my underwear. With General Tso's chicken. No way." Plus I hadn't showered in two days and my hair was mostly made up by dry shampoo at this point.

"So, throw a cute dress on, shave your armpits, and get out here. Come on, you're a lifestyle blogger. Come take some cute going out pictures! I'll even photograph you in portrait mode so you have some good content."

Damn, she knew how to get me. A good Instagram photo op was my downfall. And I did have that new LOFT jumpsuit that would be totally easy and cute to throw on. My hair could go in a top knot ... shit, I was already visualizing an ensemble.

Dropping my chopsticks with a sigh, I relented. "Fine. Give me an hour."

I hung up, not bothering to make any more pleasantries with Jill. She understood. She was one of my rare and only friends from college. She got me, and I think that's why I actually bothered to keep in touch. We both had the same sarcastic, semi-detached attitude. A love of fashion. Valued honesty.

The only difference was, she was a hopeless romantic, and I thought that love was a silly notion peddled by Hallmark.

An hour and a half later, I was already a glass of wine in, weaving my way back to my bar seat from the bathroom.

I had to admit, it was the right decision to come out. It had been too long, I was beginning to become a shut-in and I couldn't damn well run a successful entrepreneur fashion blog if all I had to write about was the newest nail polish I'd painted on my toes while binge watching *Jessica Jones*.

"These came out so good!" Jill squealed as I slid in beside her.

Jive was a cool bar/lounge just twenty minutes from my apartment, with blue and purple lighting and rhythmic house music that gave it an ethereal feel. We'd been chatting and sipping at the bar, too old for the loud dance floor at this point.

Oh, and Jill was trolling for single men in between snapping photos for me to post. I'd already loaded my Instagram Story with bites of my drink on the bar, a hot cleavage baring selfie, us dancing in a Boomerang ... you know, basic bitch kind of stuff.

"Thanks for convincing me to come out of my bat cave," I joked, taking a drink of my new glass of rosé.

"I can't let you waste away in that apartment, it hurts my soul to watch it. Plus, your tits aren't always going to look like that, so use them while you can."

A few seats down the bar, a guy caught my eye and nodded his head in greeting. He was cute, but not my type. Blond, burly, looked like a John Cena clone or something.

If I was going to have to suffer through flirting or dating, he at least had to be tall, dark, handsome and lean. A little spark in murky green eyes, a little dark hair to run my hands through.

Why was I describing someone I definitely shouldn't be thinking of as a romantic option ...

"That guys is totally checking you out." Jill says this so loud that blondie at the end of the bar can definitely hear.

"Not interested." I turn my eyes to my drink.

"Seriously? You're the worst wing woman. You could at least introduce *me*!" She downed the rest of her cosmopolitan.

I leveled her with my stare. "The last two guys who talked you up in here had wedding rings on. They were openly just trolling for chicks even though their dicks have another woman's name stamped on them. If that doesn't show you that all men are pigs, I don't know what will."

Jill rolled her eyes at me. "Okay, maybe you're right about those guys. But I know he's out there. My Mr. Right. The one."

God, I hated this whole "the one" talk. It was bullshit. No one had a soul mate. Sure, I guess I believed that people could fall in love, maybe not me, but other people. But I didn't believe it was because they had a soul mate. Being with someone was a conscious choice, one you made over and over again. Even through the difficult times, through the shit. You decided to love that person despite their flaws, not because some divine intervention came in and sprinkled rainbows and unicorns over you both.

"Hot damn, fresh meat at six o'clock." Jill straightened, ignoring me and pushing her breasts out.

I didn't even try to be sleuth. I just turned all the way around in my bar seat, looking behind me for whatever guy was about to hopelessly hit on us next.

But ... I was pleasantly surprised. Two older gentleman, probably late thirties, mid-forties, were eyeing us. They weren't foaming at the mouth, like some of these twenty-four-year-olds who approached us, but instead biding their time and politely eyeing us, calculating when to make their move.

The one that captured my interest had salt and pepper sprinkled through his dark locks. A sharp suit, not the jeans and untucked polo or button down look. He was mysterious, and my lady parts responded. Now, just because I don't believe in love doesn't mean I don't believe in a good roll in the sack. No, *that* I definitely believed in. A mutual agreement to make one another feel good, no strings attached. That was a *real* pact.

"Hi, I'm Emmitt. Can I buy you your next drink?" And just like that, sexy older gentleman was in front of me.

His friend sidled up to Jill, but I was too busy considering if I wanted to accept another glass of wine from him to really listen to their conversation.

Figuring I had nothing to lose, except for my thong hopefully, I shrugged. "Sure, why not."

"Great." He sat down on the empty stool next to me, and waved the bartender down. "Is that rosé ..."

He's waiting for my name, and so far, he's respectful so I give it to him. "Erin. And yes, it is."

Emmitt orders, a glass of wine for me and scotch on the rocks for him, and then turns to me. "I don't mean to be blunt, but you're the most beautiful woman in this bar."

Normally, that line would be creepy or make me roll my eyes. But coming from him, it sounded sincere and honest.

And made me blush. And I never blushed. "Well ... thank you. What do you do, Emmitt?"

For the next hour, I actually sat and talked to a member of

the opposite sex. And for the first time in a long time ... I kind of liked it. I got a thrill from flirting. His take on the food industry, which he worked in as a brand advertiser, was interesting, and he wasn't bougie like most guys I met these days.

After briefly considering taking him home, or letting him take me home, I turned the idea down in my own mind. I didn't feel like the awkward stranger dance tonight, learning a new body, trying to train him toward what I liked in bed. It was too much effort. Plus, I hadn't gotten waxed in two weeks.

But I did give him my number.

ERIN

The next morning, with a headache that rivaled a fucking freight train smashing through my skull, I woke to my phone buzzing on my nightstand.

"This better be God calling to take me to hell. Or maybe that's where I already am." I picked it up, my eyelids not responding to my brain's signal to open them.

"Not God, but I'll do you one better. The hottest, friendliest guy on the planet is back in the City of Brotherly Love." Reese's voice comes through the phone, and I groan.

Because instead of hooking up with McDreamy's twin last night, I was thinking about my stupid best friend and his stupid dimple. And why the fuck was I doing that?

"Good. Go to bed," I mumbled, dropping my head back to the pillow dramatically.

"Someone had too much to drink last night. You're almost thirty, remember, Er?" He chuckled.

Oh, I remembered. Mostly because he'd brought that stupid pact up and there were also crow's feet beginning to march their way across my face.

"It was the wine's fault. And the tequila's. And the martini's," I grumble.

"Jesus. I think I need to come over there and ring you out." Reese's words are supposed to come off as a joke, but instead, there is a subconscious sexual tension laced in there.

And we both feel it, as witnessed by the awkward silence that follows.

"Want some breakfast? My treat. I'll buy you a fatty egg and cheese sandwich somewhere." Reese breaks the weirdness with a brunch offer.

I roll over, mentally going over the effort it would take me to get out of the house. But I really want that breakfast sandwich.

"Ugh, just know that you're making me get out of bed and brush my teeth right now."

"T his is exactly what I needed." I bite into the bacon, egg and cheese on a multigrain bagel, and a glob of ketchup drops back onto the plate.

Reese watches me as I eat, and I can see his eyes trace my mouth. We haven't connected since he moved back a week ago, which wasn't uncommon for us to not talk and then just call the other to hang out. We were best friends after all, there were no pretenses or small talk in our relationship.

But that damn kiss had hung an awkward cloud over all of our interactions, and I hated that I had thought about it each time I thought of Reese now.

Putting down my sandwich, I was about to get brutally honest up in here.

"Should we talk about the kiss? Because I think it's put this weird, male-female friendship vibe between us and I really fucking hate it." I couldn't deal with this anymore, I wanted my best friend back.

Reese looks hesitant. "Well, what do you think?"

What did I think? I thought love, at least romantic love, was bullshit. I thought that it made people weak, and that our pact was stupid. You couldn't just arrange matters of the heart, even if I believed that marriage was a bullet-proof institution. Which I didn't. I thought, if he was asking, that kiss had sparked something dangerous in my mind. That for a split second, it had made me question what our bond really was, and everything I thought about love.

I thought that I wanted to keep Reese in his slot, the one marked best friend, and to close the lid on anything more.

"I think that we should grow up and get over it because we're too good of friends. And one drunk kiss after eighteen years of friendship shouldn't stand in the way of that. And now that you've moved back, we can go back to being assholes to each other but really loving each other underneath."

Okay, so it hadn't just been one drunk kiss. There were those other two times, that we'd never discussed. But I wasn't unsweeping those from under the rug right now either.

Reese studies me for a moment, and I'm afraid he's going to say the things that are really lurking under my skin.

I liked that kiss.

We should explore more.

Think about the pact.

But he doesn't. Which is both a blessing and a curse. "Sounds good to me. And while we're being assholes, what the heck is that shirt you're wearing? You look like a pirate."

I snort laugh, because Reese always made fun of my high fashion pieces. "For your information, this shirt cost more than one of your shifts at the hospital. And it was sent to me to wear by the department store that handles this line for the designer. So shove it."

He kind of had a point though. The sleeves were puffed on the white top that had buttons down the front and a ruffle leading to a bow all knotted up at the bottom. It was a bit extra for Sunday brunch, but then again, I lived in a city and had a frilly fashion blog, so my life was a bit extra.

"Well, it's ugly. I like you just fine in jeans and a T-shirt. Remember that camping trip we took with our dads sophomore year?" Reese laughs, his jaw and dimple dancing with the deep, jubilant sound. "You couldn't even rough it for three hours. I found you in that log cabin bathroom trying to find an outlet to plug your curling iron into."

"Camping is for psychopaths. Who in their right mind would want to sleep on dirt and cook trout over an open flame?" I shudder, remembering the horrible experience.

And remembering how much my dad had wanted to take me to do something he loved. Our relationship had been distant and stunted for the past five years, which was his damn fault. If he hadn't ruined our family, and destroyed my mom in the process, maybe I would be more lenient to have a conversation with him.

"Many people, including me." Reese finishes off the rest of his steak and eggs, patting his flat abs through his T-shirt, and I wonder where it all goes.

Lord knows this grease ball of a sandwich is going straight to my hips, which I'll have to work doubly as hard at spin class to maintain.

"All right, I think I need to go back to bed. And I have work tomorrow. Ugh."

People who use that cliché phrase, "You'll never work a day in your life if you love what you do." Yeah, well, they definitely weren't talking about me. I fucking hated my job, and most of the people I worked with. Most of them were opinionated, obnoxious assholes who threw their views around as if they were bible verses and bashed anyone who didn't fall in line.

"Why don't you quit that place? You have a steady gig with the blog, you could make it work." Reese said this as if it was so simple.

Because I'm petrified I'll fail. Or go broke. And I'm also terrified that I'll actually succeed.

I don't say any of these things as he pays the check, as he promised, and we leave the restaurant, parting ways on the sidewalk with an easy hug and little to no tension left.

But the afternoon conversation with my best friend did beg the question: What the hell was I so scared of when it came to getting what I wanted?

There is absolutely nothing better than a baseball game in the heat of summer.

The sweat of your thighs rubbing against the plastic seat, the scent of warm beer, popcorn and pretzels. It's one of the first things I've wanted to do since moving back, especially since I hadn't been able to watch my home team on TV when I lived in Dallas.

"This is the worst," Erin complains beside me.

She never was a fan of Phillies games. "Come on, I bought you a beer."

"And it's warm. And cheap." She pouts, her full lower lip jutting out.

"You've never turned a cheap drink down before. Chin up, buttercup. The mascot is about to do a dance." I stick my feet up on the empty chair in front of me.

Erin rolls her eyes. "Oh lovely, that big green thing is gyrating. You know, you have to be totally secure as a person to dress up as a fictional character for thousands of people to see."

I laughed, because she was kind of right. "Who do you think

is in there? Like, do you think some investment banker does this for fun as a hobby?"

She cocks her head to the side, a fluff of foam from the beer sticking to her lip. I want to reach over and swipe it off, like a best friend would, but it feels different now.

"Maybe it's like, a really desperate middle-aged woman who doesn't get enough attention and needs the applause to cheer her up."

"Oh, so you mean, you could be in there?" I slide my eyes to her, my gaze full of innocence that my sarcastic barb has none of.

I'm not surprised when she twists my nipple, painfully, between her thumb and forefinger. But fuck, does it hurt. "Ouch! No fair, you know I have sensitive nipples."

"That's why I love to purple-knurple you." Erin gives me a smug smile as she sips more from her beer.

I won't lie and say that my cock didn't twitch a little when her fingers squeezed my nipple. Apparently, I like a little pain with my pleasure. How kinky of me.

"Seriously though, who do you think is in there?" She ponders again as the Phillie Phanatic dances across home plate.

"Maybe it's Jaime Dornan." I jab her, knowing her secret love for the sexy actor.

Erin would never admit that she read the wildly popular romance novel for which he played the lead on the big screen, because it would mean she believed that love was possible if she scarfed down those books. But I knew she read them. This one time, I'd stolen her phone, while she tried to punch me in the balls, and gone into her Kindle app. It was chock full of romance books with shirtless men on the cover. I had never let her live it down until this day.

But mentioning another man brought me back to our conversation last week over coffee, when she told me she'd given her number out to a guy at a bar. I might've broken things off abruptly with Renée, I may be insane for crushing on my best friend, but hell if I wasn't a raging shade of green when I thought about Erin letting some random guy walk her to her apartment door after a late night date.

"You think?!" She let her nonchalant mask slip for just a minute. "Oh, you are such a tease. Maybe it's one of the former players."

"Or a madman, serial killer just trolling for victims." I patted her knee, as if to signal that we were getting too far into this guessing game.

Erin nodded. "Yeah, I think it's too much. All right, what do you have on tap for the rest of the week?"

"Saving lives, taking names. You know, all in a day's work." I flexed a muscle and she hit me in the stomach, lightly but with enough force to have me letting out an *oof*.

I liked to joke around about my job to others, because it kept me from getting too deep into the emotions. In reality, working in the NICU was emotional turmoil on the soul at all times. Even for a manly man such as myself. Har, har.

Really though, I cared for sick babies around the clock. Feeding, changing, rocking, checking vitals, supplementing with medication, alerting doctors when one of them stopped breathing, helping to change oxygen tubes, turning on heat lamps or incubators. And more. And that was just the clinical side of my job.

The worst part was handling the emotions of parents, especially mothers just hours to days off of labor and delivery, who couldn't celebrate their baby's new life because it was still hanging in the balance.

If I got into it, if I really discussed what my job was like on a daily basis, I would crumble under the toll of it. But, I did love it. I loved what I did.

"Which one of the nurses do you think will ask if you're gay first?" Erin smirked.

The question was inevitable, and she knew it. It happened in every hospital, whenever someone new started on my floor. There weren't many male nurses, and it was extremely rare to see one in the NICU.

"Who knows? But I bet you twenty bucks it happens within the first six hours of my shift."

We sit watching the game for a little, me observing the plays and her on her phone, scrolling through Instagram. Always working, that one. She worked harder than anyone I knew, both in her traditional job and for her blog. I can't say I hadn't creeped on her most recent post about the best bathing suits for summer. Tracing the outlines of her body with my eyes on the stupid social media app.

"How about you? Anything fun this week?" I ask when I feel the silence becomes stilted.

Erin chews her lip, thinking, and I think about the kiss we shared. Does she think about it at all?

"Just my shitty day job. But I did get invited to this launch for a new champagne company on Friday night, so that'll be fun for the blog. Want to be my plus one?"

I always wanted to be her plus one. I know I said I wouldn't mention the pact anymore, but how could she not see it? We spent so much time together. Even when I lived in Dallas, we texted at least once a day. I could be her plus one for life, if she'd let me.

"Of course. I mean, who else would you take? It's not like you have other friends." I stuck my tongue out at her like we were in fourth grade again.

Erin rolls her eyes. "I do, too. Ones who don't make me sit in the horrible heat, next to smelly drunks, watching a game that is so slow, it's like watching paint dry."

Some of the other fans watching the game overhear this and turn to snarl at her. I smile amiably and wave at them, trying to smooth over the egos of crazed Phillies fans.

"Are you trying to get us killed?" I hiss at her, but have to laugh at her audacity.

"It'd be better than this." She raises her beer in a cheers to me, and then laughs before downing the rest of it.

Did I mention that I hate my job?

Sometimes, when I walk into the offices of the Philadelphia Journal, I imagine I'm Milton from *Office Space*, mumbling about burning the building down.

"Morning, Carter." My boss, Mike, combs his fingers through his mustache as he not-so-subtly checks out my ass when I walk by his office.

I skirt to my desk, awkwardly bending my body and legs while trying to be as obscured from his view as possible. Maybe if I walk right along the wall, his creeper eyes won't see me.

Mike has been the editor-in-chief since I started working here, and has worn that pedophile facial hair on his pudgy upper lip for probably twice as long. He's an asshole, makes sexually explicit comments to his female staff, delegates most of his work to his department heads, and I'm not sure why they keep him around still. Oh yeah, because his family owns a share of the damn paper and he'll never be fired.

Cue my enormous eye roll and huffy sigh.

I set my purse, the violet fringe one I found in a vintage shop that had no brand label, down on my desk and boot up my computer. Savoring that first sip of coffee, I close my eyes as I sit down, trying to get my blood pressure to a sane level before all of the annoyances of the day put me into near cardiac arrest.

I shuffle through my emails, a Greek yogurt sitting on the corner of my desk, discarded, as I shake my head at all of the stupidity in my inbox.

And just as I sigh to myself, about to dive in to the mound of shit I have to accomplish today, I hear it.

That nails-on-a-chalkboard voice.

"Good morning, coworkers!" It shouts across the office, peppy and too sugary-sweet for eight a.m. on a Tuesday.

There are some people in life you're just not going to get along with. And if you're me, that is most people. I just see right through all of the bullshit, the playing dumb, the fake nice that a lot of other people don't mind. It irks me, sets me off. I think more people should be like me, the world would be a hell of a lot more honest.

"Hey, Erin. Oh my God, I think you got some coffee on your pants."

Katie Raymer walked by my desk, and I already wanted to throat punch her. The office suck up, she had bleached blond hair that was fried to a crisp, wore shirts a size too small so that the men would stare at her boobs, and couldn't write for shit. Even though she ran the paper's lifestyle section, which was the job I originally asked for when I came on five years ago.

She was my work nemesis, and it pissed me off even more that she was all, "bless your heart" to my face. Like the pants comment she just made? She was kindly trying to tell me I had a stain. She was trying to point out that I looked like a mess, and that she would never be as irresponsible as me. It was all subtext with people like Katie.

"Katie." I nodded, not even looking up from my computer.

"You know, it's so funny. Last night, I tried this new face

mask. And I thought it wouldn't work, and it made my face absolutely flawless. Like, how good is my luck? And I got it for fifty percent off at the store."

She launches into a discussion no one is having with her, that no one asked her about. And why does she always try to make her good fortune sound like a negative, as if we should commiserate with her about having gorgeous skin and full pockets?

Maybe I'm just crabby because I'm getting my period. My cramps have been at near-volcanic eruption status, and I can't stop munching on chocolate covered peanuts.

"Awesome," I mumble, trying to get her away from my desk.

"I also was watching that new reality show about the wives and girlfriends of athletes, and like ... I realized that I probably will be one of those someday. You know, with Hans playing hockey in that amateur league around here. And like, am I going to have to be one of those women who doesn't work? Because being a makeup contour specialist is not a job."

Her hands are on her hip as she rambles, both bragging and offending large groups of people, and I want to throw my hot coffee on her. No one makes me as ragey as this bitch.

"Mike, let me tell you about this piece. You'll die!" She stalks off, not even realizing I barely acknowledged her verbal diarrhea, off to flirt our boss into giving her more vacation time.

If there was anything I hated in this world, it was brown-nosers. Just kidding, I hated a lot of things. But brown-nosers were at the top of the list. I didn't get anywhere by sucking up or networking. I would rather put the hard work in, keep my head down, and be rewarded when the quality of my work shined through. Those who obtained their status by stepping on the backs of others and not putting in the effort ... that really pissed me off.

And I wasn't just exaggerating when it came to her. She

constantly cut me down in editor meetings, once stole a story right out from under me when there was no way to prove I'd done the research first, and she'd even eaten my lunch out of the fridge once. She claimed it had been an accident, but no way did you mistake two spicy tuna rolls if you hadn't brought them yourself.

The only thing that got me through was periodically checking my blog and Instagram stats, new followers, and if any companies had direct messaged me trying to partner or work on a project. I really needed to get out of here, and I would.

Eventually.

When my will to follow my dreams without a safety net won over my fears and need for a steady paycheck.

Thursday night sees me lying in bed, naked, watching *HGTV* and eating cheddar flavored crackers shaped like fish.

So, in essence, I am both an eighty-year-old and a five-year-old all at the same time. I'm boring, watching DIY shows ... but am also chowing down on the same snack my mom used to put in my lunchbox during elementary school.

My period swept in yesterday with a fucking vengeance, as if Aunt Flow was extra mad this month that I wasn't using my ovaries, uterus and all of the other parts for what they were intended for.

The couple on *House Hunters* was about to pick one of the three houses they'd seen, and I was getting bored. And full, my snacking monotonous more than for hunger now. But I mean, did I ever snack because I was hungry? And did I ever stop because I wasn't anymore? The answer was a no.

Picking up my phone from the table beside my bed, I opened up the text conversation I had with Reese in my messages.

Erin: *So, how was saving babies today?*

It took a minute for him to respond, and I scratched my boob, the skin itchy in the prickly heat of early summer. I was definitely a hot child in the city, or whatever they said.

Reese: *Ultimately, boring. Snuggled cute newborns, helped postpartum mothers. You know, all in a day's work.*

Erin: *Did you push one of epi?*

Reese: **eye roll emoji* I love that you think my job is just plugging heart arteries in elevators and having great hair to go with my scrubs.*

Erin: *Grey's Anatomy basically makes me a doctor, or didn't you know.*

I giggle to myself, because I have teased Reese constantly throughout his post-college career. I ask him any and every situation I've ever seen on the popular ABC show, and if he's ever experienced it. And he usually just shakes his head at me.

Reese: *Whatever, nerd. What're you doing, anyway? Eating Goldfish in bed while watching House Hunters?*

He knew me too well. I brushed the Goldfish dust off my fingers and went to respond. Except, when I did, I fumbled my phone, a series of actions set off by my clumsiness.

In the flash of a second, my naked chest was illuminated, the flash on my selfie camera going off. I grab for the phone, the corner of it hitting my open eye and I let out a howl, the feel of it foreign and somewhat stinging. Holding my right eye, I snatch the phone off my comforter, where it bounced and landed.

And howl again when I pick it up and see just what I've done.

A seedy, close up shot of my right boob, and part of my left, sent directly to Reese. *Fuck. My. Life.*

I wish, in that moment, that I could unsend a text message. That I was crafty enough to hack a network, or dashboard, or whatever kind of shit needed to be hacked to not allow Reese to see that picture.

Fuck. He probably had already seen it.

An accidental tit pic ... who the hell does that even happen to? Me, that's who. My fucking luck, I was that creepy guy on the Internet who sent random people shots of his dick. Except that this was a shot of my nipples.

Sheer hot mortification runs through me as I see those three tiny bubbles pop up. I want to look away, but I can't, my train wreck laid out there for both Reese and I to see.

It's not even a *good* picture of my rack, my boobs are all lopsided from lying down, and strands of my hair are caught in my armpit.

What is he going to say? Should I type something preemptively? Maybe say that it's a shot of someone else and I was totally pranking him? Dear lord, I wanted this panic fluttering through my stomach to go away.

Reese: *Well, damn, if you wanted to marry me so bad you should have just said so. No need to convince me with sexting. Even if it's not even good sexting.*

Erin: *Ha-ha, jokes on you. That's not me! Gotcha.*

Reese: *Peas, I'm not a moron ...*

Dammit. *Dammit.* At least he could joke about it. But now, after we'd gotten that awkward kiss out of the way and had settled into being best friends who lived in the same city ... now I had gone and sent him my boobs.

I picked up the phone, embarrassed but not wanting this to turn into anything weird again. With a wave of embarrassed nausea, I tap the screen to call Reese.

He picks up on the second ring. "Is this a booty call? Because I've seen the goods, and listen, the lighting was a little dark if you're going to put that up on the blog ..."

"Shut up! I didn't mean to, okay? My fingers had Goldfish dust on them, I fumbled my phone ..."

"Sureeee, we'll go with that." Reese cackles on the other end. "Do you text all of your friends pictures of your boobs? Trying to figure out if you should invest in new bras? I'll tell ya, I think you're good there."

"Oh my God, I'm going to murder you. Stop it now, I just ... wanted to call to tell you it was an accident and that you should delete this moment from your brain, and we can go on being best friends and making fun of each other about which house the couple picks at the end of *House Hunters*."

I can still hear him laughing as he answers. "Fine, fine. But it's going to take one of those memory eraser pens, like in *Men in Black*, for me to forget this one."

"Good night, Reese Maximus." I said his middle name, a jab because I knew he hated it.

"Hey, not fair!" He starts to argue with me, but I hang up, not wanting to keep this bickering going.

Flopping back on my bed, I cover my eyes in exhausted embarrassment.

Clearly, I needed to put a lock on my cell camera or something, to avoid situations like this. I'd certainly learned my lesson.

No texting and Goldfishing.

My new apartment was a full-on bachelor pad.

A black leather couch, beer mugs where the drinking glasses were supposed to sit in the kitchen cabinets, two stools tucked under the counter instead of a kitchen table, and I'd only forgone the pool table because Erin had given me the death glare.

For two years, I'd been on and off living with Renée, who did the decorating. Before that, I just let whatever girl I was dating take over the apartment I'd been renting. By the time I moved home to Philly, I'd donated most of the furniture, lamps and wall art to a women's shelter. They'd been appreciative, but gave me a funny look as I dropped off all of the feminine decor.

"Seriously? Your shower is so dirty, you should talk to management by the way, and all you care about is the TV?" Erin walked around the place, inspecting it with a container of Clorox wipes in hand.

I fiddled with the cable box, smacking it like that would actually get it to work. "The baseball game is on in an hour."

"So what?" She pounces on the fridge, opening it and wrinkling her nose.

I thought that my explanation would be sufficient, but apparently, she did not understand that television was the most important part of a man's move-in process. "Never mind. So, when are you moving in?"

For a few weeks now, I'd been badgering her intermittently about the pact. In my hotel room at the Residence Inn, which I'd been shelling out money for until I could find a decent place to rent, we'd spent more time together then we had in years. It was incredible, and everything that I'd forgotten I needed just clicked into place.

"Um, try never. I won't be your next keeper." She scowled, cleaning a vegetable drawer she'd removed from the fridge.

"My keeper? Do tell. Sounds kinky." I tried to program the remote again, but it wasn't working.

"You're constantly rebounding, Reese. You move from one relationship to the next because you can't possibly be single." I'd forgotten how blunt Erin could be.

They stung, her words. "That's not true ..."

She cocks an eyebrow at me, an arm moving to rest a hand on her hip in a motion of attitude. "You probably didn't even pick out the pair of pants you're wearing."

I looked down, noticing the navy joggers I wore. That my girlfriend before Renée, Denise, had bought for me.

"Sure, maybe I am a bit codependent." Erin raises her eyebrows. "Okay, a lot. But it's not because I don't live my own life. It's because I like living it with someone else. I enjoy leaving decisions up to the couple, having to talk and compromise. That's what a relationship, and companionship, is. Getting joy out of living with someone else, out of merging your two lives together. We can't all be self-sufficient robots like you, peas."

Erin points a finger at me, her brown eyes turning a midnight black with her annoyance. They always grew darker when she was mad.

"Don't start that peas and carrots stuff with me, Reese. I just think, it would be good for you to be single for a while."

I continue to try to hook my TV up. "And *I* think, that we should honor our pact and get married. You need to know what it's like to have to rely on someone. I think that would be good for you. Hell, we're already best friends. We know how it would work."

Erin's eyes don't lose their stormy look. "You're insane. Clinically, I believe. I think we need to admit you. Does your new job have a psych floor we can put you on?"

"Come on, peas. It'll be just like in *Gump*. Friends forever, stood by each other for years, harbored feelings. And then, in the end, they fall deeply in romantic love. Plus, I've seen your boobs now. Even if accidentally."

I won't lie, she has a great rack. And I'll never let her live down sending me an accidental tit pic.

She harrumphs at me. "Except that you and I never harbored feelings. Except those of annoyance. You annoy me like a little brother."

That one stings. Is she lying, denying? Or does Erin really feel that way? Because ... I've always had feelings for her. Ones I've rarely acted on, and never dared to tell her about. There were only two times I came close; a New Year's kiss hours after midnight, and in a hot tub on her twenty-first birthday in Atlantic City. Bottles of champagne were present for both, as was disappointment. We'd never talked about either.

I brush it off again now, because what the hell would she say if I told her I'd loved her for the better half of my life? "I'm not your little brother."

Erin laughs, mocking me in a singsong voice. "Younger by two weeks and five days. I'll never let you forget that."

"I'm a responsible fucking man, don't forget that. And you'd be lucky to have me."

"You nurse sick babies back to health for a living. Of course you're a man. And a catch," Erin admits in defeat, but shrugs me off.

"So, then, why won't you honor our pact? We've already established I'm a catch, a pretty damn good-looking one if I do say so myself. I can take care of kids, so I'd be a great dad. And it'd be better than falling in love, because we would be partners. Best friends."

"Do I have some sort of Cinderella-esque midnight expiration date stamped on my forehead? That was a pinky promise we made when we were fifteen!"

I catch a lock of her long corn silk hair in between my fingers. "If you don't marry me by the time you're thirty, you might turn into a pumpkin."

Erin's eyes level me. "I think that only happens to pure as snow virgins. And I think we both know that I am not of that variety."

My blood boils at the same time it heats; both with lust for her and jealousy that other men have been there before me.

"And I think we both know that I could give you so much better than you've ever had." I turn on the charm, knowing that she's always had a weak spot for my dimple.

If only I could take her in my hands right now, mold them to her body and explore every dip and crevice. That kiss has haunted me, for weeks I've been a starved man. I've thought of little else when I lay my head down on the pillow, staring up at an unfamiliar ceiling.

"Who needs a man? I can masturbate and change a light-bulb by myself." Erin's voice is low and her eyes are concentrated on my dimple, and then flick to my lips.

"Can I watch?" We're centimeters apart now, the gravitational pull of our attraction, which she won't admit is there, bringing us close.

"The masturbation or the lightbulb?" Her voice is a hair above a whisper.

I shrug. "Either. I love a woman who knows how to be handy."

My voice conveys the double entendre, and my hands shake as I try not to touch her. I've already kissed her once without permission. She has to be the one to make the next move. I can only coax her so far, push her so much without revealing exactly what I was trying to do. I knew Erin, and she had to be the one to make the decision. If I forced the issue, she'd bolt.

"Just think about it, okay? Really think about it." I tried to keep the desire and desperation out of my voice.

I'm not sure why I was pursuing this. Or, maybe I did. Maybe I'd known all along that in the end, it would always be me and Erin. That instead of running from Renée and Dallas and my life, I was instead coming back to the place and the person I was always meant to be with.

"Fine." She backed away, breaking the moment. You could cut the sexual tension with a knife. "I'll think about it."

"Give me sex kitten."

"Okay, now give me dewy-eyed love."

I flutter my eyelashes, trying to look off into the distance like I see a long lost love.

Fat chance, I can only fake it until I make it so much.

My friend James kept clicking, photographing the fifth outfit I'd changed into for this shoot. I was creating content for a summer wardrobe blog post that would be going up later this week, and he was my go-to photographer. James understood style, makeup, the mission of my blog and brand ... and was a self-declared fabulous gay man with, "fashion better than my blow jobs."

No really, he'd actually said that to me once.

And although we had been friends for two years, ever since I met him at an amateur bloggers happy hour, he didn't *know me*, know me.

Or how fucked-up I really was.

Being a child of divorce, especially one whose parents decided to implode their marriage later in life, will fuck you up six ways from Sunday. And my parents picked the jackpot of horrible times to announce their separation ... a week after I'd gotten my job at the Journal.

What should have been a time for celebration, proud family moments, nervous energy and first day jitters was spent in complete grieving mode.

For me, at least. Morgan curled into herself and into her husband, too distraught to deal with it and already established in her marriage. She could focus on her little family unit, while I imploded.

Maybe that was why I'd always had a bad taste in my mouth when it came to my job. It started in such a bad mental state for me personally, that I don't think the position or the workplace ever stood a chance. I spent my first week crying in the bathroom when I knew that no one else from the building was in there.

Mom was an emotional wreck; walking around the house in a bathrobe like Mrs. Havisham. I'd still been living there, my search for an apartment put on hold as I picked my own mother up off the bathroom floor every night before bed.

That was how I learned about the death of love. Even before that, I'd always been a bit awkward when it came to dating and relationships. I never felt emotionally connected to men, considering for a short period that I might be gay. But after a one-off experience in college, I came to the conclusion that while beautiful, women weren't for me.

No, I was just simply built with a tougher exterior. I didn't fuss, I was never boy crazy.

But after my parent's divorce, that outside shell hardened to the point of steel-enforced concrete. That's what watching a heart physically break will do to you. I could see the beating organ in my mother's chest just stop. The sounds that she would make, the deep, soul-wrenching sobs that would wrack her body.

I simply never wanted to go through that.

Which was why I couldn't think about giving the pact a real shot. Reese should get it, he knew me better than anyone. But he'd still asked me, even after we'd said we'd leave it alone.

My insides burned with that question, with his plea to consider it. With confusion for everything that had transpired these past weeks, months. I'd gone from blissfully ignorant, living my single life in a sarcastic, glittery bubble, completely fine that my best friend lived hundreds of miles away.

And then he had to up and move back, and shake my whole life as if I were a magic eight ball that could rewrite the future.

"These are going to look great in your new blog post for summer." He turns the camera to me, scrolling the images.

He's not lying. He always manages to make me look five pounds skinnier, which is why I kept paying him to shoot my content. "Damn, you're right. And I am actually still squealing over the fact that Nordstrom wants me to do this blog post as sponsored."

"Just remember me on your way to the top, honey." James waggles his fingers at me.

We're at a rooftop bar in Center City, flowers and greenery trying to mask the fact that we're sitting floors above an urban jungle. I love it here, with the hot sun beating down on my back, some fruity, alcoholic drinks on standby, and a bag full of my latest fashion finds waiting to be paired together and photographed. This was me in my element, doing the work that wasn't like work at all.

I could see the Instagram posts now; the summery collection posed on my body in front of rows of flowering trees, over-looking skyscrapers. It would be edgy but flirty, summery but sophisticated.

As we finish up, James packing his camera bag and me folding the last of the outfits, patrons start coming in. They say that being a lifestyle blogger is all fun, parties, clothes and booze, but really, it's early morning calls and sneaking in shoots when locations weren't occupied. I'd done some fact-checking on this place for a piece in the Journal, and I'd gotten to know the bar manager a bit throughout the process. That's why she'd agreed to let me use it for one of my blog posts, as long as she didn't spill the beans that I had a blog to my day job. She said that was fine, as long as I was okay coming to do the shoot at six a.m., before the restaurant opened on a Saturday.

I think I owed James an arm and a leg, or a Kate Spade bracelet, for his trouble.

"Thank you so much, buddy, I really owe you one." I hug him before we begin to walk toward the elevator back downstairs.

"Yeah you do. Making me get up at the ass crack of dawn. But hey, there are some gorgeous shots in there, so it helps my portfolio, too."

"As if you need help with your portfolio. You're the best photographer in the city."

"Erin?"

Fuck. That voice. I'd know that voice anywhere.

I turn, and there she is, in an obnoxious magenta fit-and-flare dress that does nothing for her figure. "Katie ... hi."

I try to shoulder the bag full of clothes on my hip around my back, so that she can't quite see it. Not that James and his camera standing next to me aren't obvious. Clearly, we've been doing something here, and her powdered shit nose is trying to sniff out what it is.

"Oh my lord, I trekked all the way up here for brunch with the girls and they're running late. But it looks like you got an early start ... who's your friend?" She bats her eyelashes at James, and she's certifiable if her gaydar isn't pinging right now.

But there she is, shamelessly flirting with a man who could care less about her boobs.

"We did, thanks. We were actually just going, have a good brunch." I might be a bit callous in that moment, but I didn't care.

She'd never done me any favors, and Katie Raymer was the last person I wanted finding out about my blog. I may sound paranoid or harsh, but she was just one of those women. One of those women who didn't grind for other women, who would use information against them to watch them fail. I'm not being dramatic when I say that she'd stab me in the back, and the front.

Katie is stuttering as I push past her, and my hasty dismissal probably doesn't do much for getting her off my scent, but I'm exhausted from shooting all morning and want to spend the rest of my Saturday watching Hallmark movies and painting matte lipstick swatches on my arm.

In the elevator on the way down, James speaks first. "Who was that awful cow? And why was she salivating over any ounce of information you were about to give her?"

I roll my eyes, breathing a sigh of relief that we're out of her presence. "A coworker, and yes, she's definitely awful."

"Girl, you need to quit that hellhole. *Now*."

I fan my face. "Yeah, that's what people keep telling me."

A new mother, bloodshot eyes barely able to contain the tears about to burst from her eyes, is wheeled into the NICU.

I see this every day, a fresh off delivery pair of parents who are scared and have no idea what is going on. It isn't natural, that they're in here. When they tell you you're having a baby, you imagine holding that tiny human in your arms and sleeping with it on your chest.

They don't want to be here. They don't want to see me. So I try to brighten their day, and the short hours they are allowed to see their child, just a little bit.

"Welcome to the hospital's best wing. Male nurse, reporting for duty." I salute them, weighing the mother's personality simply because I've seen so many and know how to play situations.

She looks at me, cracks a smile, and chuckles. "I guess if you're having a baby boy, you'll want someone who knows how to deal with that anatomy."

She's joking with me, and I thank God she is. "Very true. You must be Nicole, with baby boy Graden?"

"That's our boy." The father looks like he's trying to keep it together, and is doing just barely better than her.

"Let me assure you, we're doing absolutely everything we can to get him better and out of here. Now, I know you don't care about the tour. Just know you have to wash and put scrubs on each time you come in, but other than that, you can come anytime of the day or night to visit. Except from two to three p.m., because that is the nurse shift change. Let me take you to Graden."

They look desperate to hold him, but their little boy will probably be in the incubator for another two weeks before that happens. I watch as they sit, smiles spreading across both of their faces as they reach their hands into the gloves to touch his tiny arms and hands without skin-to-skin contact.

I've been working at CHOP for three weeks now, and already, their technology, process, and staff is light-years ahead of any other hospital I've worked in. Even after being in this field for almost seven years, I was learning new techniques and procedures.

And there was even another male nurse, as well as two male doctors on the NICU floor.

"Are those the parents of the baby boy who came in this morning?" Preston Graham, one of the two male doctors, asks.

We'd become bros, even though he was technically my superior and younger than me at the same time. A resident, Preston was a calming force in the sea of estrogen, and smarter than anyone I'd met. And that was saying a lot for this field. We'd geeked out over our love of comic books when I'd been watching one of the Avengers movies on my phone in the break room. I had a feeling that he didn't get out much. And I said that because I literally never saw him leave the hospital.

"Yeah, they seem like they're keeping it together. They'll be okay." We looked on at them as they smiled at one another, and then looked back down at the baby.

"By the way, Lucy asked me if you were straight." Preston had a no-nonsense way about him ... which was probably why I'd liked him so much as we worked together more.

"Shit, I owe Erin twenty bucks." I walked with him, taking the vitals of the babies on the row he was observing as we went.

"Huh?" He laid his stethoscope to the chest of a baby girl who was due to be discharged today.

"My best friend, she always bets me how long it will take for someone in the hospital to ask that. You wouldn't get it, you're a doctor."

Preston looks at me, his head cocked to the side. "I wouldn't be gay because I'm a doctor?"

The guy was damn smart when it came to medicine, but his common sense was a bit lacking. "No, no. You're a doctor, therefore no one assumes you're gay. There is some weird vibe about being a male nurse ... people automatically think you like guys. And there is nothing wrong with liking guys, if you do, but, I'm straight. And well, stereotypes suck. I guess that's really the point of it."

"Ah, I see. Well, I can tell her you're not, if you want me to. Why do I feel like I'm stuck in a bad after school special right now? Maybe you can give me a note to give her next."

Okay, so apparently the guy wasn't as street dumb as I thought he was. "No, that's okay. Keep them off my scent. She's asking because she wants to see if I'm straight and single, in which case, she'll probably want to go out."

Preston pulls the chart off of one of the incubator beds, studying the status reports on the baby. "That's quite cocky of you."

I shrug. "It's happened many times before. Cocky? Maybe.

Accurate? Definitely. And I'm fresh off a train wreck of a relationship, so no thanks."

Preston looks up, his close-cropped blond hair reminding me of some kind of orderly military man. "I don't date, out of principle. It's messy, unnecessary, and I just don't have time for it."

He reminded me eerily of Erin. "Good man. I think I'll take a page from your book."

Except that I'd asked my best friend to consider marrying me on the grounds that we'd make a better partnership than actual lovers would. And she hadn't responded yet, or spoken to me in three days. That was practically a century for us, and I was scared I'd finally spooked her. Why was she acting like the man in this situation? Noncommittal, aloof, it was like she was ghosting me after a one-night stand. Yet, we hadn't slept together and the one kiss we had shared ... she wouldn't admit to even feeling anything.

"Hey, listen, we should go get a drink. Watch a baseball game at the bar across the street."

A lot of my guy friends from home had either moved away, gotten married, or hadn't kept in touch. I needed to hang out with the bros, do some fist pounding, beer drinking and just get my goddamn mind off of women and their mysterious ways.

Preston looked at me cautiously. "I usually study at nights ..."

"Come on, man, you can take one night off."

His shoulders slump, almost as if he's being punished. "All right, fine. Maybe one night next week. But I'm too busy this week."

"Well don't sound so enthused. Next time I won't put a gun to your head." I laugh.

"No, I want to. We'll catch a few ... quarters. Cheer on the guys on base."

Jesus. This guy apparently lived under a rock, he didn't even know that baseball had innings. Well, at least I knew that if he ever had to tend to my kid, his whole life and knowledge was about fetal medicine.

"Good, stop making me laugh. I pee every time I get up to stand, let alone contract my muscles in merriment."

"That sounds truly awful." I tilt my head to the side, regarding Morgan's enormous belly.

I scored a blogger discount to Pottery Barn Kids for my sister and brother-in-law, and we'd done the room in neutrals and pinks, with a small elephant theme running throughout. Although, I'd thrown a unicorn stuffed animal in her crib. Kid had to be a little unique, let her freak flag fly.

Morgan was sitting on the floor, looking like a buddha, folding small clothes and putting them in the small drawers assigned for my future niece.

"That's not even the worst part. I woke up the other morning with dried crust all down my arm. I thought maybe my nose had been running in the middle of the night. Then I took off my tank top to get in the shower ... nope, turns out my boobs have started to leak. It was freaking milk, crusted all down the front of me. I feel like a damn cow and the baby isn't even here yet." Morgan rolled her eyes, the same shade as mine.

"I don't understand why anyone would *want* to be pregnant." I truly don't, but then again, I value my freedom and sanity.

Morgan smiles, in that big sister way that tells me I'm about to hear some sappy speech.

"Because as much as it's gross and you feel terrible, the other half is amazing and wonderful. When I feel her kick, it's pretty incredible. Like … Jeff and I made this tiny human being that is going to pop out and become a part of our family. And when I think about her, what is she going to look like? Then there is the sex drive, *out of this world*." She whispers the last part.

"Ew, I do not need to think about you, or Jeff for that matter, having sex." I shudder.

"But seriously, this is all worth it, because at the end, I'll get a baby." She rubs her belly like the baby can actually hear her.

Who knows? Maybe my niece can hear her. "Yeah well, I'll stick to fun aunt status. And I won't lie, I've gotten the cutest clothes for that little lady. And I've gotten a ton of traffic on the blog doing so. Mommies are a big audience."

Morgan nods, folding the tiniest pair of overalls I've ever seen. "I saw that, very clever, Aunt Erin. When are you going to give your two weeks at that hell hole?"

Unlike some people who knew about it, my sister believed full force in my dream to become an entrepreneur slash full-time blogger. And when I said some people, I meant my mom. Who I loved dearly, but she thought that having a job meant you got in at eight a.m., did your traditional, professional duties, and went home at five p.m. And that you did that in the same company for twenty-five years. She didn't understand that that wasn't the way the world worked anymore.

"I think you're about the fifth person to say that to me this week. Reese was hounding me the other day, and James, my photographer friend, asked too."

Morgan pulls my hand to her stomach. "Oh my God, she's kicking."

We both listen for a minute, feeling the distinct pitter-patter of tiny baby feet pounding against the lining of her uterus. It was freaky and amazing all at the same time.

She drops my hand a few moments later. "How is Reese since he moved back, by the way? Still with that southern monster?"

Morgan has made it known, as has mom, for the last ten years that she thinks I should date Reese. I haven't told her about the pact, ever, and I haven't told her what happened when he came back for the interview. Or that he seriously wanted me to consider marrying him. She would flip her fucking lid, she'd be so happy.

"No, he's single." I don't say more, out of spite.

Morgan waggles her eyebrows at me. "Maybe it's finally your time."

Jesus, why did everyone around here think that some magic fairy had come and sprinkled dust over my best friend and me, leading us to our happily ever after and rose colored glasses? An idea strikes me, and I feel guilty about holding back from Morgan recently. She's my sister and we talk about everything, why shouldn't I talk to her about this?

"How did you know you wanted to get married? I mean, didn't Mom and Dad turn you off to the idea forever?" I question, thinking about my own current ... situation.

It wasn't even a situation, because I hadn't even told Reese if I was going to give this stupid pact a serious shot.

Morgan looks at me, a bunch of little baby headbands in her hand. "Er, sometimes ... I think you took the whole divorce a little bit rougher than I did. And sometimes, I think you give Mom and Dad too much credit. I'm the older sister, so I saw more than you did. They weren't perfect."

"They were perfect to me." Her words etch away painfully at my heart.

She sighs. "I guess to us, yes, they seemed that way. But that's a different story. Anyway, I knew I wanted to get married because ... life without Jeff wasn't a life. Everything is better with him. The days, my attitude, going out to dinner, walking in the park ... everything. When he asked me to marry him, even before that, there was just this spark between us when we were together that I never wanted to go without. It was this feeling, I can't describe it, but it was like ... this was the person who was put on this earth just so I could spend time with him. And you're going to say that sounds corny, and it might very well be, but that's seriously how it felt."

I digested her words, chewed them over in my brain. The only person I felt remotely like that with was Reese. Maybe ... maybe all this time I'd been mistaking this spark that Morgan was talking about as a friendly connection. When really, Reese was the one who was put on this earth for me to spend time with.

But in the same breath, I had to roll my eyes at my inner-thinking cap. I didn't believe in soul mates or fate, not on principle. Morgan and Jeff were great together, but did I believe she could be happy with someone else if she wasn't with him? Yes, I did.

"I don't know if I'll ever feel that way." I say it sadly, because I know how wonderful it must be for other people.

Yes, I'm a colder person than most. I am judgmental before I am kind, my core sometimes seems poisoned. Was I born this way, or was I conditioned to be harsher? It wasn't as if my sister or parents were like this ... I often wondered why I was.

But anyway, I may be cold, but I'm not unfeeling. I know that when others are happy and in love, they must feel this sort of bliss. But like someone attempting to jump out of a plane and mentally not being able to ... or like a writer attempting to spit out a chapter but being blocked ... there was something holding me back. Like my brain could complete it, but my heart could not get on board.

"I think that when you least expect it, something will click." Morgan eyes me, and then goes back to folding a little pair of orange pants that only a baby could get away with wearing.

16

I'm not sure why we decided not to date each other. Why a romantic relationship was always off the table.

Maybe it was because we'd met so young, and our parents were friends.

Maybe it was because we teased each other relentlessly, and spent so much time together that, originally, we knew too much and therefore the idea of anything happening between us was subconsciously off limits.

But as we grew up, I think something between us shifted. I think that question hung between us, but neither of us would acknowledge it for the fear of messing up our friendship.

And now, I've said something. After the two, now three, physical connections we'd had, it was time to say yes or no. It might ruin our friendship if nothing panned out, but it had to be brought up. Erin hadn't given me an answer or even an indication that she was considering our pact, and my time of not pushing her was almost up.

We only had two and a half months left until her thirtieth birthday, and about three months until mine. It might seem like a silly, child's game I was playing, but something in me felt the need for closure on this. And if the answer was no, I prayed that our friendship was strong enough to withstand putting us through this.

I hadn't told her that Renée had texted me last night. Or two days before that. Opening up my phone while Erin is at the coffee kiosk getting out breakfast, I read the conversation again.

Renée: *Hey, we haven't talked in a while. How is Philadelphia?*

Reese: *Hey. It's been an adjustment, but work is really good. And being close to my parents is nice, too. How have you been?*

Renée: *I've been okay, thinking about you a lot. I don't like where we left things, babe.*

Reese: *I'm sorry that I left the way I did. I truly am. But Renée, you had to admit that things were over for a while. I want you to be happy, I want us to move on.*

Renée: *Don't pull that move on stuff with me. We were in love, you don't just shut that off. I haven't. Can you honestly say you have no feelings for me?*

Reese: *I'll always feel something for you. We were together for a long time.*

Renée: *Then you do. I think we need to talk about this.*

Reese: *Renée, I … maybe another time. I just got off a night shift and I need to go to sleep.*

Renée: *I can call you later this week.*

Renée had always been the kind of girl who got what she wanted. But with me, I'd never fully bent under her stilettos. I hadn't even really wanted to hear from her, but at the same time, I owed her some explanations. And I wouldn't lie and say I didn't still think about her. She was a huge part of my life for over two years. With how difficult Erin was being about my advances, it was no wonder why I was leaving the door ajar with Renée a little.

Erin set us up, coffees and donuts set out on the bench in between us. The air was warm, but not as humid as it had been when I lived in Dallas. Early morning runners, moms with strollers, and couples walking their dogs loitered around, no one talking but just exchanging smiles.

"I missed this old pastime." She grinned, and I knew she meant it.

Throughout our years at separate colleges, we'd meet in the park on Sunday mornings and people watch, catching up about life and unwinding. It was our time, and we developed this game as part of the ritual.

"Okay, who are we starting with?" Erin rubbed her hands together as she took a big bite of a chocolate frosted.

I leaned back, crossing my right leg over my left knee and taking a gulp of my black coffee. Twelve-hour night shifts at the hospital forces one to drink coffee strong and quick.

Almost everyone in the park at nine a.m. is minding their own business. Working out, strolling, chatting quietly to a companion or just sitting like Erin and me.

And then there is the disheveled woman, carrying her shoes with lipstick smeared across one cheek, and the mark of a round nightclub stamp clearly inked on her right hand.

"Bingo." Erin says it before I am even able to get my thought out. "Okay. Her name is ... Heidi Green. She works in communications, but really wanted to be a sideline reporter through college. Keeps trying to find 'the one,' but doesn't understand why these fuckboys don't call her back after drunkenly falling into their beds after nights at Live or Halcyon. Drinks almond milk lattes and secretly loves presidential autobiographies, though she'd never tell her basic brunch friends that."

I nod. "Nice touch with the autobiographies, maybe you're

not just a heartless witch who doesn't give people the benefit of the doubt."

Erin scowls at me. "Come on, add."

We played this game, making up life stories for people as we ate donuts and coffee. Kind of like people-watching cops, except we had no badge, no gun, and no honor.

I tapped my chin, trying to think up a positive angle. We both had our roles; I was the good cop, and of course Erin was the bad. Our personality types were so reversed for what our gender stereotypes should be. I was often told I was too nice, polite and not jaded enough. Usually I was told that by Erin. And my best friend? If she were a man, she'd be a quintessential "fuckboy," as she referred to them; hard to get, cocky, could be a show off. Why was that such an attractive quality in people, whether they were male or female?

"Okay ... Heidi actually likes her job, acting as a public relations rep for authors at a publishing house. She gets free books, and that's damn skippy with her. She goes home on the weekends, to the Mainline where her parents live with their miniature pinscher. Not really into reality TV, crime dramas are more of her thing, and she binged *Mindhunter* last week. She is a romantic, which is why she sometimes finds herself in these situations, and is tired of dating after all these years. Or, she is just a boss who sleeps with guys and then discards them, because she's an independent woman who just needed an orgasm."

Erin chokes on her coffee when I say orgasm, and I'm pleased with myself for making her proverbially blush. It's funny, because I'm semi-describing her.

"Heidi also prefers tea over coffee, and can't listen to a thunderstorm without opening all the windows and watching the rain."

"Oh, come on. How come you always turn these into nicefests? People watching is supposed to be funny and sort of mean-spirited." Erin pouts and takes another bite of her donut.

I sling an arm around her, conspiratorially. "You were just blessed with an extra nice friend to outweigh the devil inside you."

She sticks her tongue out at me. A minute later, she's typing away on her cell as I continue to relax and watch the activity of the park as it comes to life.

I never understood why most of the population have their noses stuck in their electronic devices all the time. Wasn't it far nicer, and less stressful, to sit on a bench and sip coffee and breathe in the morning air?

"What are you doing?" I study her as she balances a coffee in her hand at an awkward angle, her phone aimed at the watch and bangles on her wrist.

Erin doesn't look at me, just concentrates. "Trying to take a picture for Instagram."

"Do you have to document every single minute of your life?" I roll my eyes.

"You do know that it's weird you live almost off the grid? And yes, my followers expect to know what I'm doing. It's part of my brand." She has her shot, and begins working on the lighting and hues in some app on her phone.

I watch her as she poses, trying to get the perfect shot. Her blond hair blowing, that hint of sassiness in her brown eyes ... I've always seen it, but it's hard not to realize why all of her followers hang off of her every post. She's magnetic, even when she's shunning the world away.

She's addicting, even though she'd rather be alone and aloof.

I snatch her phone out of her hand, pocketing it. She squeals and tries to grab across my lap. I hold her shoulders, bringing us nose to nose.

"Your brand today is to sit with me and relax. Can you do that?" We're too close for comfort, and I think I've stunned her.

Because her big brown eyes are just staring widely, mirroring my own, and she slowly nods.

I release her, electricity crackling between us.

I guess that time and space I was giving her is officially done.

A fter our coffee in the park, we're walking through the city, the morning chill burning off as sweat drips down my back.

And then, on the horizon, is every girl's sanctuary. Nordstrom Rack.

"*Oh*, can we go in?" I probably have heart's in my eyes, like that emoji.

Reese groans. The one major dissension in our friendship ... he hates to shop. I learned about it after we were already solidly friends, so I couldn't disown him because of it.

"She don't believe in shooting stars, but she believes in shoes and cars." He chuckles to himself, that damn dimple popping out.

"Don't quote Kanye to me ... but, yes, I do believe in shoes and cars. Those are tangible things that make me happy. Shooting stars? Those are for Disney princesses and five-year-olds."

Reese looks at me, and I see the pity in his eyes. It's one of the first times I've ever seen that look pass between us, and I don't like the way it makes my skin heat with shame.

But he doesn't launch into anything. "Fine, we can go in."

I do a little hop and a skip, because I freaking love Nordstrom Rack, and pull out my phone to start Instagram Storying as we walk in.

"Again with the phone?" Reese asks, annoyed.

I turn the camera on him. "This is my best friend. He is complaining that he has to go on this impromptu shopping trip."

I hit send on the story, and two seconds later, my phone starts dinging with direct messages.

Your friend is hot!

Is he straight?

Is he single?

Can you do a try-on session for us?

I need some affordable romper options, please!

Can you post your friend's Instagram so I can stalk him?

"My followers love you." I type away, answering messages.

I have a strict policy for myself that I answer all direct messages. Well, the non-creepy ones, that is. I never answer date requests or porn bots ... because, well, you get why.

"Awesome. I try to stay anonymous from social media and you just screwed that all up." He throws his hands up, his muscles flexing through his olive skin.

His light brown curls, which are shorter now than when he was living in Dallas, bounce as we move, and I envy how wavy and perfect they are at the top of his head. That moment in the park, the smell of donuts and fresh coffee in my nose, with our faces so close together ... it shook me a bit. We hadn't really touched since the kiss. Best friend air hugs didn't really count when you'd been doing them for years. But when his hand touched mine, and his other arm laid around my shoulder, and those greenish-brown eyes, like mud in a cerulean sea, looked at me ... I felt it.

The spark.

I must be a goddamn crazy person. As I've thought more and more about the pact, and what Morgan said, and how Reese has been on me about it, I'm actually softening to the idea.

Not marriage, of course. That's fucking certifiable. But, about maybe dating him. Looking at him in another light.

We walk through the store, and I pick up a dress, a pair of shoes, a floppy hat. And then I see a teal short-sleeved button down with gray arrow patterns. It would look great on Reese, and I throw it over my arm.

"What is that?" He eyes me suspiciously.

"Nothing." I shrug, innocently.

"I'm not trying anything on. And I'm not buying clothes. I hate this as it is." He's pouting, his full lower lip jutting out.

My phone keeps going off, and I check Instagram to see almost a hundred new messages about Reese or my impromptu shopping trip.

And then an idea strikes me.

So many of my followers have boyfriends or husbands, and they often ask about male clothing brands that I like ...

"Will you do a try-on session with me for my Instagram followers?" I smile like a cat who ate the canary, sweet and trying to hide my intentions.

Reese's face shuts down. "Nope, don't even think about it, peas ..."

"Carrots," I use his nickname, trying to soften him, "come on, pleaseeee?"

He shakes his head. "Absolutely not."

"If you do a men's try-on session for me, I'll let you take me on a date." I can't even look at him when I say it, it was so weird.

But this try-on session is something I want, and the date is also something I've been thinking about, so I'm about to kill two birds with one stone. Or well, kill them with fashion.

Reese's hazel eyes widen, and then set on me. Something that I can't name passes between us ... something that in our years of friendship, I have never felt between us before.

"Fine. You better get that camera ready, I'm about to give you the best damn show you've ever seen." He grabs the clothes out of my hands, and I scurry about the rest of the men's section, grabbing at pieces I know will work well on him.

We head for the dressing room, and two women look at us as we walk into a stall together.

"They think we're going to have sex in here." Reese says it, and I thought it but didn't voice it.

How odd, this subtle shift. A tingling starts low in my belly.

I bring up my phone and start storying. "Hey guys! I'm here at Nordstrom Rack with my best friend, Reese. Say hi, Reese."

To his credit, he's taken his shirt off, abs of steel winking back at the camera. And me. I hadn't seen him naked in a long time, I realized. Probably since we'd gone to Wildwood two years ago.

That tingling intensifies. The adrenaline of videoing him, contributing a new segment for my followers, and also about our future date had started a prickle that travels from the top of my head to the tips of my toes.

Direct messages were already pouring in, but I kept putting up stories, starting a new one each time the short video ran out of time.

"Okay, so right now, Reese has on this teal button down, perfect for your man for summer. It's only thirty dollars, and comes in a bunch of different colors." I narrate while Reese struts around with his best *Blue Steel* look on.

He addresses the camera in the next video, laughing like this is a joke. "It breathes really well, and matches my eyes, don't you think, ladies?"

Little does he know that this shirt will probably sell out from their website and this location. I'm not cocky, but I do have two hundred thousand followers. And growing. Also, they're all fawning over him, which I won't tell him. Because, you know, don't want his ego getting too big.

In another minute, I'm looking as he pulls off his gym shorts and stands before me in boxers. This shouldn't be weird, he's my best friend. I've seen him run ass naked into the ocean on prom weekend. But now it was different ... and damn, did his ass look more sculpted at thirty than it did at eighteen? Men got all the good aging genes.

"Now, these are chinos that fit perfectly, he's wearing a size thirty four. So nice for brunch with friends, or even work if your man's office is casual dress."

I kept shooting as he tried on item after item, never putting up a fight. He was funny and charming for my followers, and I knew that I'd have to bribe him into doing this again. I'd even snapped a few photos so I could put a blog post together.

After we're done, I'm typing down the brands in my phone, and Reese bends down so his face is in mine.

"You owe me a date, peas."

Another day, another shitty eight hours at work.

I'm hiding out in the bathroom, trolling celebrity gossip sites and counting my steps on my Fitbit app. I'm one of those people who uses a bathroom break and turns it into a mini-lunch hour, because I hate my job that much.

Sighing, because I know I've been gone too long, I get up, situate myself, and go to wash my hands. As I stare at myself in the mirror, I think about what I always think about ... Shoes and the City.

My blog constantly consumes my thoughts; new ideas for posts, how I can generate more followers, which partners I'm teamed up with this month.

"Oh man ..." I groan, spotting a big fat whitehead on my nose.

How long have I been walking around with this? I was so distracted and agitated, thinking about yesterday and Reese wanting to collect on the deal I'd made him for a date.

"I know your secret." Katie walks into the bathroom, catching me completely by surprise.

What the hell is wrong with this girl? I've just peed and need a moment to pop the pimple on my nose, and here she comes, invading the bathroom like a bat out of hell. Fangs and all.

But my heart rate picks up, and I just know she's talking about my blog. My hands and the back of my neck start to get clammy, and I hang on to the counter for support. Bad move, she sees that I'm nervous.

"When were you going to tell me you were so into fashion?"

Fuck. Fuckity, fuck, fuck. This is not good. For a split second there, I thought she was going to say something else. I thought she was going to say that she found my stash of candy in my desk, or that she'd seen me somewhere with Reese and thought I was dating someone. But I should have known better. The minute she saw me at that rooftop photo shoot, I should have known it was coming down to this.

"It's really not something I share with a lot of people." I try to give a generic answer and scoot past her, but she blocks my way.

Her puggish nose is sniffling and salivating over my weak positioning in this conversation. "Not something you share? Girl, you have two hundred thousand followers! I should have featured you in my section a long time ago. How come you never told me?"

Um, because we're not friends. I don't say it, but she has to know that's the obvious answer.

And she's only saying she'd put me in the section because she wants to find out more about my blog, to get the dirt on me and try to take away a little bit of my success and claim it as her own. See, Katie is the breed of woman who cornered me in the bathroom instead of on the newsroom floor because she's sneaky and dirty. She wants this to be her little secret to hold over my head until the minute she wants to expose it to everyone. This isn't a friendly girl-to-girl chat, this is a standoff.

"Like I said, I don't talk about it with *colleagues.*" I assert the word colleague, letting her know that we are not, in fact, friends.

"Oh, honey, you really should let me profile you. What a piece that would be for the lifestyle section, and think of how many new followers I could help you get!" Jealousy seethes from every pore, she's so desperate now.

God, I hate this bitch. She thinks she can help me? When I've built this business from the ground up, spent all the waking, and sleeping, hours of the day grinding for it so that I could finally start making money and gaining influence. Yeah, I don't think so.

"I don't think so, but thank you. And if you could keep this to yourself, that would be great." I push past her, not even waiting for a response.

The air in the bathroom was choking me, and I gulp in stale office air as I make my way back to my desk. Katie is definitely not going to keep this quiet for long, which is why I start to develop a plan in my head.

Maybe it's time to take the advice of the people who love me and want to see me at my best. Am I brave enough to do it? Maybe.

But with Katie now holding my fate in her grubby little hands, I had to act first.

I'd wanted to take Erin out immediately after she'd agreed to a date, so she didn't have time to back out.

But with my work schedule, and being the newbie even though I had three more years of experience than almost every nurse on my NICU floor, I got stuck with some terrible shifts. Three overnights this week had me feeling like Frankenstein coming to life as I woke in the middle of the day on Friday.

It was four p.m., and I had three hours until our date at the swanky Italian restaurant I'd made a reservation at. I was going pure, traditional class for our first night out as a possible romantic couple ... and Erin never could say no to a good bowl of penne vodka. I guess having a leg up on all of your date's favorites wasn't a bad position to be in.

Checking my phone, I see the text from Preston waiting for me.

Preston: *Still meeting for a drink?*

That's right, I'd promised him we would meet at the bar close to the hospital. Crap. Well, I could still meet him. The restaurant wasn't far from the bar, and I could use a little pregame drink to calm my nerves. Why the hell was I so nervous about going on a date?

Because it was with Erin.

I would be lying if I said that I hadn't thought about this happening. That I hadn't imagined what it would be like. Christ ... I sound like a little girl daydreaming about her wedding day.

Reese: *Yeah man, let's meet at six?*
  Preston: *Sounds good. That way I can be back at the hospital and sleeping off my beer at seven.*

Jesus, I needed to get this guy out into the world more.

Feeling like warmed death, and smelling like it too, I got out of bed and started to make my way to the shower. Until I realized that my apartment looked like an actual pig lived in it. I was worse than a fat farm animal.

Blame it on my hectic work schedule, or the fact that for the past two months I hadn't entertained anyone, much less a woman. But I believed we made our own luck, and if I cleaned up my apartment thinking that Erin would come back here for an after dinner drink and some more exploration like that kiss we shared many months ago, I was going to have to straighten up.

Running around, I quickly threw cups and plates into the dishwasher, ran a Clorox wipe over the bathroom counter, made my bed, and threw my dirty laundry in the washer. Mom would be proud, and it smells less like a barnyard in here than when I started.

Never one to really primp, I showered quickly, picked out a pair of slacks and a button down, ran my fingers through my hair, and winked at my reflection.

Okay, that was too cheesy, tone it down. I nod, confident. Better.

I'm out the door at five thirty and making my way across Philly to meet Preston for a drink.

"Why can that guy slide into that other guy's leg like that? He's going to break his femur." Preston muses.

I shake my head, amused but slightly exhausted from trying to explain the game of baseball to a guy who clearly has done nothing in his life but read medical textbooks.

"Sliding is allowed in baseball, and most of them go head first to avoid injuring the other player. But that was a clean slide, and he was safe." I finish my beer, wanting a second but holding back because I don't want to be buzzed at dinner.

He sighs. "Well, I always thought sports were dangerous. A great example of how the human body can bend and break, but dangerous nonetheless. Although this seems gentler on the body than football, now that is just moronic. I've seen the case studies for CTE, why anyone would put themselves through that brain trauma is a mystery to me."

"I don't disagree, but you don't know what some of those players need that paycheck for." For some of the guys, it's their way out.

But that is a discussion for another day.

"You want another round?" Part of me wants him to say yes so that it gives me less guilt about having another.

"I shouldn't. I'm going to go sleep this one off in an on call room so that if I'm needed, I'm already at the hospital." Preston finishes his beer.

"Do you even have an apartment? Or do you just sleep in the hospital?" I joke.

"Oh, I have a place, but I don't think I've been there in about a month."

I love my job, but this guy takes it to another level. "I know we are both passionate about our jobs, so I hope this isn't a weird question but ... why do you work so hard?"

Preston looks down at his clasped hands, and I can feel the mood shift. "This may be heavy for an after work drink ..."

I clap him on the shoulder. "Hey, man, we're friends. You can talk to me."

He doesn't look at me, but he starts to talk. "When I was eighteen, I got my girlfriend pregnant. We were young, in love but very young. We were still excited though, as only children can be when they have no idea how hard life will be for them after that baby comes. I promised her so many things ... but when the baby came, a boy, there were so many complications. He had mosaicism for trisomy 2, a disease so rare that the free clinic we were forced to have her obstetrician appointments at, because our parents were not going to help, didn't even catch it. The baby was basically stillborn, and the hospital had no idea how to handle his case, or even care for him to try to improve his health and give him a fighting chance. It really broke me. It ruined our relationship ... although who knew if we would even be together if the child were healthy and alive. And so I vowed to dedicate my life to finding cures for these horrible diseases. To give these little lives a chance. To never have to see another parent in the state that I was in, to give them hope that their child would be okay."

I had been completely wrong about Preston, and I internally scolded myself. He wasn't cocky, he wasn't a science nerd just in this for the intense research and accolades. He really believed in what he was doing, and was ultimately, trying to make a difference in one family's life.

I squeezed his shoulder and then dropped my hand away, stunned at his honesty. "Wow, man. That is ... wow. Thank you for being so open with me, you're a stronger human than I'll ever be."

We sit in silence for a minute, digesting his words. "Sorry to put a damper on our happy hour ..."

"No, man, you're not. It's good for me to hear, to understand a little bit more of your motivation. Seriously, thanks for sharing with me. If anyone can change the lives of those newborns in our units, it's you."

I truly believed it, too.

"Enough about me ... don't you have a date tonight or something?" Preston gave a shaky laugh, rattling the grief and despair off his psyche.

I look down at my date night attire and smile. "I do, probably should get going soon."

He nods, standing and stretching, wearing his blue scrubs that he never seemed to take off. "Who's the girl?"

Erin's face pops into my mind, and my stomach drops. "My best friend, actually. We've known each other since we were kids, and only recently decided we might turn it into something more."

"Could be weird." He shrugs, leading the way out.

I agree. "It could be. Or it could be awesome."

20

I pulled out Erin's chair, the lilting of soft Italian music filling the air as the lighting dimmed for dinner.

"Thank you." She said it politely, almost like we didn't know each other.

I don't think this woman had used manners toward me in, well ... forever.

"You're welcome." I smiled, trying to put her at ease.

To her credit, she'd dressed the part as if she was going on a date with someone she was trying to impress for the first time. A black dress that hugged every curve, soft waves in her blond hair, the kind that I would like to tangle my fingers in. Her shoes looked sharp enough to murder, or dig into my waist ...

I was getting way too ahead of myself, and tried to discreetly readjust myself under the table. For her, these thoughts might freak her the fuck out. But for me ... I'd been having these since we were twelve and had gone in the pool for the first time before eighth grade. She'd been in a red floral bikini and I'd nearly creamed myself, I was such a horny tween.

Her brown eyes were dark and mysterious, and I knew that I had to break the ice.

But Erin spoke before I could. "You're not going to order for me, are you? I hate that, when guys do that. It's cheesy and unromantic. Like, I'm a human and am fully capable of reading this menu and making a choice without the assistance of a man, thank you very much."

Chuckling, I lay my hand on hers. Maybe that was risky, but she doesn't move it. "I wouldn't dare get between you and your food. Although, I know you, and you're going to get the penne vodka."

"Maybe I won't, just to spite you." She raises an eyebrow.

"Don't deny yourself what you want just to make a point." After I said it, I realized how well it applied to us.

The waiter came, offering us wine or spirits, and we ordered two glasses, white for her and red for me.

"Straight out of 'Scenes from an Italian Restaurant,'" I quipped.

"Remember when you thought that it was *Brender* and Eddie?" Erin started to laugh.

"It definitely sounds like he says *Brender*! I thought it was about two boys who were the popular steadies."

We chuckle as the waiter sets our glasses down, and we each take a big gulp before he comes back with bread and asks what we want. I go with the chicken parm, I'm boring and traditional when it comes to meals. And Erin goes with the penne vodka like I'd predicted, and looks damn happy about it.

Once he leaves, we both practically down our wine, alternating between people watching and awkwardly smiling at each other.

"This is a little weird, you have to admit it." She tucks a strand of hair behind her ear.

I laugh, tension breaking over me as I relax. "Okay, so it's weird. It's not a normal date, I basically know everything about you, even when you had your ugly phase in middle school."

"Hey! I never had an ugly phase."

I tilt my head. "Come on, you had braces and you had tried to dye your hair pink but it came out bleached and fried instead."

"Okay, fine, that was bad," she concedes. "But seriously, Reese, do you ever think there can be romance, not that I believe in it, between us? We know too much."

God, how I wished I could take all of those preconceived notions of love out of her head. She was only getting in her own way, so much hurt and scar tissue left from her parent's divorce.

"But maybe that's a good thing. For once, can you try to swallow the negative thoughts? Look at the bright side, I'm not a creep—"

She cuts me off. "Debatable."

I raise an eyebrow and then go on. "You don't have to worry about if I keep dead bodies in my basement. You know where I come from, that I have a good family. You know that I don't have weird habits, like collecting my toe nails or gambling until I'm twenty thousand in debt. I'll treat you right, I'm good-looking, won't get too drunk to the point where I can't get us home safely … just let go, Erin. Don't let it be weird and it won't be weird. And if you try to let go hard enough, maybe it can be a little romantic."

She blinks slowly at me, and I think it's one of only a handful of times that I've seen her speechless.

"For instance, I forgot to tell you how beautiful you look tonight." I say it quietly, with no sarcasm or teasing.

And it's so quick that you might miss it if you didn't know her better … but, Erin, she blushes.

Right there, I can feel it. That something that's always been bubbling beneath the surface with us. Like a dormant volcano always on the edge of erupting, something was just keeping it from exploding.

The pact, maybe it would be the thing to set us over. To set the world around us on fire.

21

He walked me home from the restaurant as the streetlights came on, the summer heat making the air buzz with humidity.

It was like a scene out of *Lady and the Tramp* or something. Except I'd never share my pasta with him. Pasta was too precious.

"Do you have work tomorrow?" I didn't know what to do with my hands.

This was a date. If it was good, which by all standards it had been, we would be holding hands. But my arms limply hung by my sides, like wet noodles that didn't know how to act.

"Nope, free to sleep in. Or well, catch up on sleep. Night shifts beat the hell out of me, you know that." Reese looks at me, his eyes tracing my body.

Was I supposed to heat under that stare? Because I did. How had I not noticed any of these things before? It was like my mind subconsciously blocked these feelings until I checked a box to turn them on, and then they'd suddenly started. Like notifications on an app, they were vibrating straight to my heart.

It was a short distance to my apartment, but I'd drank too

much, and I was wobbly on my feet. Stumbling, I steadied myself.

But Reese had caught it, his hazel eyes missing nothing, and his warm hand enclosed mine. How many times had I touched him? Hundreds, and yet I'd never registered the topography of his skin. How his fingers eclipsed mine, the way his hand wasn't rough, but wasn't smooth. How our hands meshed together, the way it felt good to have skin-to-skin contact. It had been a long while since I'd been with a man.

Ew, been with a man? Who was I, some corny rom-com character? And I realized, in this moment, yes I was. He was going to walk me home, I was going to fumble my keys. He would step in and help, and then slowly, our eyes would lock.

"Er? Where is your head?" Reese and I had stopped walking while I was having a silent freak out.

Looking up, we were in front of my apartment building. "I was just thinking how cheesy a swoony good-night kiss at my front door would be. The building tension, the fumbling excuses."

Reese smirks. "So let's not do it that way."

Before I can ask what he means, his palms neatly cradle my jaw, and his lips are on mine. I'm surprised, letting out a squeal of shock, but he drives right through my reaction, holding me in place so that he can properly kiss me.

And properly kiss me he does. Moving our mouths in tandem, my body adjusting to his without my brain even being conscious of it. My knees actually may go weak, my stomach drops ... like I said, it's been a long damn time since my body was attended to.

But this is Reese. This man who just so blatantly went for what he wanted, no asking, no excuse or foreplay or flirting. He wanted to kiss me, so he kissed me. It was sexy, it was strange ... I was extremely turned on.

But underneath that arousal was a sensual longing. Reese was kissing me like he'd imagined doing this for a long time. Like he'd thought about it, and was finally getting a test drive on the real model. Like the training wheels had been taken off, and he was allowed to fly free.

It felt like hours that we made out like teenagers locked in the closet during seven minutes in heaven. Except that we were standing on a busy Philadelphia street. I think someone even wolf-whistled out a window.

When we finally broke off, I couldn't catch my breath.

"So, can I call you again sometime?" Reese's nose was resting on my nose.

I got that shivery, goose bump feeling that ran down my spine ... the one that all of the girls get in those cheesy rom-coms. Lord, why did I feel like this? Why did they even invent feelings to be had like this? Nothing good could come from it.

"Maybe," I finally said, not wanting to play his sarcastic game, but also feeling weird about *wanting* to go on a second date. With my best friend. Who had seen me puke on the sixth grade field trip.

One more squeeze of his hand and I let go, turning to walk inside. We didn't say bye, or that we'd call each other tomorrow. I didn't look back, but I knew Reese waited until I got into the elevator inside before he turned and walked home. Or more likely, called a cab.

While I washed my face and put on the four anti-aging creams I was currently testing, who knew if any of this shit worked, I ruminated.

I was so conflicted, I felt more confused than when I watched *Pink Floyd: The Wall* for the first time as a kid because my parents had forced me to watch "real music and art."

On one hand, it was one of the best dates I'd ever been on.

We'd laughed, joked, the only awkward tension felt like ... flirting. Flirting, with Reese, how insane.

But at the same time, it hadn't felt like a date. I was comfortable, ate pasta instead of salad, didn't shrink away in embarrassment when he pointed out I had parsley in my teeth.

Was that what it was supposed to feel like, when you really liked someone? Like you were eating dinner with a best friend, rather than a guy who was silently fat shaming and image shaming you? What a novel concept.

And that kiss. God, that kiss. I wasn't one for heart-eye emojis and teddy-bear feels ... but even I could admit that I'd never been kissed like that.

I fell asleep that night like I'd overdosed on NyQuil, but I hadn't. My brain was just so heavy with confusion and kissing hangover that it knocked me out.

Morgan called me the next morning, to talk about plans for the baby shower that she wasn't supposed to know about, and I found myself breaking. Finally.

"I went on a date last night."

Silence from the other end of the phone went on so long that I thought maybe we'd gotten disconnected. "Hello? Morg?"

"No, yeah, I'm here. I was just trying to catch my breath from that bomb you just dropped on me. Warn a pregnant girl, please. I can barely suck in a lungful as it is. Okay, now who is this guy? You never date."

I shuffle my feet in my slippers, the blush pink fuzzy slides so cute for summer. "Um ... Reese ..."

This time, there is no silence about what I hear. "WHAT!?

You went on a date with Reese? Is this a joke? Are you punking me?"

I blow out a breath, knowing that this would be a thing and just allowing her to spew every thought that jumps into her head. "Are you done?"

"Not in the slightest. What the actual fuck, Erin? When ... I can't even form a sentence. You might send me into early labor."

"Don't even joke, Morg. And if you'll calm down, I'll answer anything you want to know." I have to sit down for this.

Plopping down on the couch, I stare out the window at the perfect, summer-blue sky as Morgan grills me. I explain about what happened with the kiss when Reese came home for his interview, about the pact that I never told her about, and then everything leading up to last night.

"So, you agreed to go on a date with him? You don't even date, not even guys who aren't your childhood bestie. Not saying I don't love this, but what made you change your mind?"

My sister always showed me the mirror, I could always count on her to never beat around the bush.

I shrugged, even though no one could see it. "I guess ... I just, I love Reese. I do. He's closer to me than even some of my family now, excluding you of course, and I could never lose him. Part of me just agreed because I don't want to hurt him and he seems truly interested in the pact. But after the date ... Morg ... he kissed me. And, I don't know. I can't say it wasn't weird, but I also can't say it didn't feel like the most right thing I've ever done in my life. God, that sounds like a fucking Hallmark card."

She sighs dreamily on the other end of the phone. "I think it might just be the most right thing you've ever done. I've told you for years that I thought Reese was *the one* for you. And now my dreams are coming true. It's straight out of a fairy tale. If your fairy tale also involved shoes and a lot of emotional baggage."

"Hey, don't talk about my shoes that way. Yeah, I'm a regular Meghan Markle." I rolled my eyes.

"All right, I gotta go, my bladder is going to explode and Jeff promised me a foot rub that I need to collect on. But I love you, I'm so happy, and don't you dare keep anything like this from me again."

She hung up without waiting for me, and I collapsed back onto the couch. I didn't want to be Meghan Markle, I didn't need the princess hysterics and unicorns and rainbows.

But maybe I would be okay with a two-bedroom apartment that I shared with a handsome fellow. But only if he did the dishes, because I hated that shit.

For a couple of summer's when we were growing up, the Carters and the Collins rented a house down at the Jersey shore in Wildwood.

The week was filled with too much sun, sand in all the wrong places, family cookouts on the rooftop deck, the sensation of the ocean as you slept, the boardwalk, and ice cream until we were about to throw it up after the Tilt-A-Whirl.

We hadn't rented a house down here in nearly two years, because of my move, Erin not being able to get time off, and Barbara's divorce. This summer, we were a thin bunch. Without Erin's dad, awkward, and because Morgan and Jeff were so close to having the baby, it was only myself, Erin, my parents and Barbara.

Even though it wasn't the larger family affair we usually had, we'd still had a fun week. Too much sun, eating until our bloated stomachs could barely walk back from the boardwalk. My mom and Barbara were almost done with their thousand piece puzzle, just like they'd done every summer we came down as kids. My dad and I had gone crabbing one morning, and all of the girls had gone shopping on the boardwalk during the day yesterday.

But this morning, I'd set up something special for Erin and me.

"This is the 'fun morning activity' you planned for us?" Erin's eyes were cautious and skeptical.

I presented the tandem bike as if I was showing off a car she were about to win on a game show, but clearly, I wasn't selling this idea well.

"How fun will this be? A little workout, a little talking, a little sunshine ... it's like your cycling class but actually outdoor and not in some manufactured sweat lodge where a steroid-user screams at you to peddle faster."

"Just because you don't exercise and look like that, doesn't give you the right to shame us mortals." She scowls, pointing to my exposed abs.

I subscribed to the thought that when one was at the beach, shirts and shoes were not required. So, shorts it was, while Erin wore a sundress that seemed to float around her, making her look like even more of a beach angel than she usually did when we were down the shore.

We'd spent time together down here, kind of testing the waters ... literally. While our parents read on the beach or walked around town, we'd spent our days together, walking and talking, or listening to music as the ocean waves played second fiddle. I'd walked her to her bedroom door each night, burning with the fire to lead her inside but knowing I had to take this slow. Our "dating" was actually going well, I couldn't rush her.

I had, however, kissed her. Twice. Once on the beach in the morning, after a run we'd taken together. And once when I'd said good night outside her door, all of the parents already asleep. I'd gently pushed her up against the wall, and laid my lips on hers until we both could barely breathe. I'd been hard as a steel pipe when I'd walked away, hobbling to my room just next door. Had she heard me collapse on my bed, jacking myself off to the daydream of her hand on my cock?

It was strange, exciting, familiar and hot all at the same time. We knew each other so well, but not in this light. Not as lovers ... which was a cheesy word but I didn't have any other definition for it.

"These peddles are too big, my feet keep slipping off. And you aren't keeping in rhythm with me!"

"You know what they say, peas, it's not about the size of the boat, but the motion of the ocean." I turned around and winked, almost throwing us off balance.

"Pay attention! You're going to get us killed." We went over a particularly rough stretch of boardwalk and Erin squealed.

Me, I just prayed that my nuts weren't damaged beyond belief. This tandem bike thing wasn't the gentlest on the family jewels.

"This is a lot more work than I thought it would be." I was sweating, and we were working against each other.

"Was this supposed to be some test to see if we could work together? Because I think it shows that we're failing," she quipped.

"I think it shows that we're both strong personalities who can peddle together or alone, when we so choose." I served her back with a glass half full.

Erin stops pedaling, and suddenly the weight is shifted to my front half of the bike, wobbling us. "I decided that I'm tired and you can peddle me, like I'm Cleopatra."

I laugh. "Anything for you, my queen."

After our ride, a sweaty hour up and down the boardwalk, we go for funnel cake, devouring the powdered sugar treat. So much for exercise.

The day ticked by slowly. We lounged on the roof, Erin doing some picture editing on her computer of photos she'd taken over the week in Wildwood. Some fashion shots, a beach blog she'd informed me, some of the landscape and architecture. I'd followed her blog over the years, hell, I'd been the one to help her buy her first website domain, but watching her work was inspiring. Erin was so dedicated, and she was really *good* at what she did.

As the sun went down, I asked her to take a walk on the beach with me.

We walked parallel to the waves, her in a big sweatshirt with the word Wildwood on the front, me in a Phillies pullover I'd had for years. I watched her in the moonlight, and wondered what was going on in that head. I'd known the woman for over fifteen years, and I still had no idea what she thought about.

Reaching for her hand, I went to lace my fingers in hers, but she pulled away. A dagger went through my pride, making my ego shrink back, and I huffed.

"Why aren't you taking this seriously?" I watched her braid her long blond locks nervously, my eyes tracing her hands every movement.

Erin sighed, and I watched the waves retreat back, taking the sand beneath my feet with it. "Because I don't believe in this. Marriage. Love. You should know that."

I should be listening to her, but the way her eyes sparkled in the moonlight, it was distracting. I'd felt her hips the other night when I'd kissed her, I knew what was under that sweatshirt. I shouldn't have picked the beach to bring up this discussion ... I would never win with this beautiful woman in front of me, and alone.

"I do know that ... I know that you put this unrealistic stamp on it." I move closer to her, needing to touch her.

Maybe if she lets me touch her, I can change her mind.

But just as it feels that we're at some peak, about to dive nose deep into this argument, or whatever we're having, we're interrupted.

"Erin! ERIN!" Erin's name was being hurtled down the beach, frantic on the wind.

That was my mom's voice, what the hell was she doing out here? I looked to Erin, and it could only mean one thing if my mother was screaming bloody murder the way she was.

Neither of us even spoke, just sprinted back up the beach, our legs burning by the time we reached the wooden stairwell that led back to the house.

"What is it?" She held my mother's arms, her eyes panicked.

"Morgan ..." My mom had tears in her eyes.

And I knew. Immediately, I knew. You couldn't be in my line of work and not realize that anguish, the unknown when it came to a woman going into labor early.

Because of course that's what happened. My mom wouldn't have interrupted us for anything less.

"She's at the hospital, Jeff called. The baby is in distress ..." My mom was motioning with her hands, like that would help explain anything.

Erin began to run, to where I don't know. I chased her, because I knew all rational thought was out the window at this point.

"Mom!" She screeched as she threw open the French doors of the sun room on our rental.

"Erin. Oh God, we have to go. She's in labor. It's too early. Oh, the baby ... Jeff called ... how, what?" Barbara was frantic, pacing and throwing things in bags and crying.

I calmly walked to the table, grabbing my keys and wallet. We'd come back for the other stuff later, right now, none of it mattered.

"Everyone get in the car. I'll drive you to the hospital."

23

ERIN

Premature.

Respiratory distress.

Ruptured placenta.

All of these words meant nothing to me, rattled around in my brain like food I could not chew, and just wanted to vomit out so that I'd feel better again.

Mom was softly crying in the corner, finally breaking down after we'd come out from seeing Morgan. The doctors had told us we could stay in the family waiting room, since she needed to rest. My sister was in almost as bad of shape as the baby was, and she had been delirious and weeping when we'd tried to talk to her.

They'd knocked her out with a blissful cocktail of drugs. I wondered if they'd hand that out to all of us. Because right now, I'd really rather go to sleep.

That unfamiliar tugging sensation pestered my eye sockets, and I knew I had to find somewhere private before I broke down. I did not cry. Ever. In front of anyone. It was weird and oddly private to me to have tears run down my face, and if I was going to give in to it, I was not going to commiserate with my mother, who couldn't seem to be strong enough to get through this with her daughter.

Walking frantically, like I was a five-year-old who had to pee really bad and had held it too long, I searched the corridor for somewhere private. The hospital was basically desolate at this time of night, and I saw a door labeled utility closet and quickly snuck inside.

And there, among the mops and brooms, I lost my shit. Uncontrollable shakes wracked my body, snot and tears mixed until I could barely see.

My niece ... she was barely the size of my hand. Two months early, not breathing on her own. I'd never seen Morgan so distraught. She was the stronger one, the more responsible one. If she couldn't emotionally handle this, how could I? And the baby, lord ... please save her. Make her better. I just wanted to keep yelling at everyone to make her better.

The door suddenly opened and I froze, my breakdown only halfway through and tears dripping from my chin onto my sweatshirt. We'd driven here from Wildwood with nothing but the clothes on our backs.

"Er?" Reese's voice was soft, and it nearly made me cry again.

"I'll be right out." I tried to clear my throat of emotion, but it broke over the words.

"Oh, peas ..." He moved farther into the closet, he could almost see me.

I snapped. "I said I need a minute. Just ... get out, Reese."

My voice was colder than I wanted it to be, and he took a step back as I turned my face away.

"I can't see you cry? Oh, that's right. Forgot, you're the woman with ice in her veins." Now it was his turn to sound harsh, but the undertone was hurt, that I wouldn't let him comfort me.

"I can fall apart and put myself back together all on my own, thanks. I'm not a damsel in distress. I need a damn minute, and then I'll be out."

Looking down, I wait to hear the door click. But a second later, after I hear no shuffling of feet or knob turning, I look up.

Only to see Reese coming straight for me. Before I can react, his lean, strong arms are around me, pulling me into his chest. He's taller than I am, by a foot or so, and if I wasn't wriggling like a caught fish, I would fit nicely into the crook of his neck and shoulder.

But I am. Struggling that is. "I said I didn't need your comfort, Reese."

My voice breaks and I scold myself for letting anyone see me like this. I've only allowed him to witness my tears on one other occasion, and that was when I found out my parents were getting divorced.

"And I don't care." He's stronger than I am, and pins me against him.

"Let go of me, Reese. Please." It's a plea, and I know I'll break if he doesn't turn around and leave right now. I don't want to be vulnerable, I don't want him to be my knight in shining tinfoil.

"Stop pushing me away. I'm not going anywhere. I'm here for you. Right here for you." His hazel eyes meet mine, and then he hugs me into him.

His warm, strong chest, the softness of his T-shirt pressing against my cheek, I am too weak in this moment to do anything but give in. I sob, whole-hearted belly sobs that shake my body silently. So deep, so utterly sad for my sister and my niece and my family, that the despair swamps me. I don't know that I've ever cried this hard, not even over my parent's marriage dissolving.

Reese just cradles me, kissing my hair periodically and whispering that everything is going to be okay.

"How do you know?" I hiccup between sobs.

It's Nancy Kerrigan-esque, I should basically start bleating "*Whyyyy*?" but he simply holds me up and lets me empty my tear ducts on his shirt.

After a few minutes, I collect myself, wiping my eyes and snot on the back of my hands. And once I have, I back away, wanting to squash any vulnerability I just showed him.

"Don't do that, I know you too well." Reese is usually a laid-back guy, but his voice commands respect in this moment.

Am I a horrible human being if that turned me on? When my sister's life is in turmoil, I'm standing in the middle of a hospital, and he is the man who used to be a boy that saw me pick my nose?

"Then you know me well enough to know that I would never willingly do that in front of you. You should have left." I turn up said nose ... which I definitely do not pick anymore.

All at once, he is not the Reese I know. Some dominant being occupies his body, his eyes turning hard, all of his muscles locking up as he walks me backward, and my butt bumps a supply shelf. I'm acutely aware now that we are hiding out in a broom closet in the middle of this hospital, *his* hospital.

And even though it's so wrong, I shouldn't be focusing on my inner-horniness at a time like this, a little jolt of electricity travels right down to *South Florida*.

His arms bracket my head, trapping me. His eyes pierce mine, and I can see a restrained swallow travel down his throat. There is so much sexual tension in this small space, I feel like the cleaning products are going to start exploding. We'll be making out while covered in Windex and Clorox.

But just as Reese dips his head, actual sparks almost shocking us as if we are both conducting static, he stops himself. Straightens. Touches his palm to my cheek.

"You should get back to Morgan. I'm going down to check on the baby. I won't leave her side, I promise."

And just like that, he turns, leaving me standing amongst the janitor's supplies, with blue balls and more emotional anxiety than I came in here with.

24

Working a night shift may throw off your internal clock until it felt like jet lag was pulling you under, but I kind of enjoyed the quiet hours on the floor. Most nights, the babies slept and there was only crying for food or a diaper change. Some of these shifts, I did get an emergency or two where one of the babies would stop breathing or need extra attending, but all in all, night shifts were actually quite nice.

Halfway through my rounds of cleaning up each babies' crib area, putting away unneeded towels and stocking diapers, wipes and medicine, I saw her sitting there, in the rocking chair, just holding her daughter's tiny hand.

I walked overly quietly, trying to be respectful and gauge if I should approach her. Just as I'm about to turn away and give them their moment, Morgan turns and smiles a small smile.

"Hey, Reese's Pieces. Come on over and see Carina." She lays her other hand over her daughter's stroking it.

Of course I've seen Carina. I've been rounding on her for almost a week, and I've been giving special attention to her case. Nagging the doctors, trying to get Preston to see what he can do to treat her faster and allow them to get discharged. But even I know it's going to be a while. Babies who are born at twenty-eight weeks don't just get to go home.

"Hi, Carina. It's nice to know your name," I say when I walk over, looking through the plastic incubator walls. "How are you doing?"

Morgan glances up at me for a split second, and then it's back to her daughter. "We're okay. Tired, fighting, but I'm just so glad she's made it so well this week, Dr. Graham says she's doing better."

Preston had been personally helping with Carina's case, because I'd asked. "There is no better hospital or doctor you could find to help her get stronger and get out of here. I promise."

Morgan's eyes become misty, and I know she's hurting. "I know that ... but it still doesn't help at all. I'm still bitter and feeling responsible. I feel robbed that I don't get to have her in my room, that they cut her out of me and I couldn't lay her on my chest. I feel like a failure as a mother, and I've only been one for a week."

She begins to sob, and I go to her, allowing her to cry into my scrubs. This is the side of the NICU that I hate, although I know it's necessary for me to have a job. Seeing the mothers break down, or try to be extremely strong for the babies, it's torture. But I'll be here, especially for Morgan, who is practically family.

"You're doing an amazing job. You're here for her, in the middle of the night. A person wouldn't do that if they weren't an amazing mom." I hug her back.

She sniffles and collects herself, looking up. "Thanks, Reese. It's good to have you in our corner."

"I'll do whatever I can." I turn to check on some more of the babies, but really just to give her more privacy with Carina.

"Sit with me?" She looks up at me, hopeful.

It's quiet, and I'm right here if anything happens. Right now, this is the most important job. "Sure."

Morgan pats my knee as I pull up a chair. "So, you want to marry my sister, huh?"

I gasp and choke on my spit. This was not about me comforting her, it's a reconnaissance mission. "You Carter sisters, Jesus."

"Come on, you knew I knew." She smirks.

"Fine, firing squad. Ask away."

Morgan shakes her head. "This isn't an interrogation, don't worry. I'm just happy, you should know that I've always wanted this. Girl and boy best friends, my ass. I know you've crushed on her since the first time you saw her. The only one too blind to see it was Erin."

"I guess the jig is up, huh?" I hang my head, smiling.

She looks at Carina, at her tiny finger. "When are you going to put a ring on it? Because we can both drag her down the aisle kicking and screaming if we team up together. She'll thank us in the end."

I shrug, unsure. "She still doubts everything about love. About a relationship ... especially one with me. She hasn't straight out said it, but I know it has to with your parent's divorce. She has this idea that love isn't real and that even if it is, she knows me too well to feel that way about me."

"Even though you've kissed." Morgan tips her head to me, as if to say that yes, she knows *everything*.

"Even though we've kissed." I grin.

"I think you need to push her more. Break her out of that ice bubble she's freezing in. You guys were made for each other, honestly, I'm glad you made a stupid pact when you were fifteen, just so that it could pan out now and finally make you guys be together in the way that you always should have been. Oh, and when you do go pick a ring, she wants a round cut diamond with a halo of diamonds around it, plain rose gold band."

Morgan turns back to Carina, and I know I should get back to work. "Thanks, Morg. It means a lot."

"Just go make a bride out of my sister. She's always been yours."

25

ERIN

I spend the next two days with Morgan and Jeff, fetching whatever they need, helping her work her breast pump, grabbing them lunch in between shifts to see their little girl in the NICU. It's a gruesome schedule; pump, eat, sleep, visit the baby. And by the exact time they finish one of those, it's literally right onto the next.

They're exhausted and run down, Morgan has a freak out every hour, and the doctors and nurses are concerned that she is going to fall into a postpartum depression. I have barely seen Reese, he's been working doubles and triples to make sure he fulfills his promise to Morgan and me to be there for our baby girl at all times.

It's been such a whirlwind that I haven't even given anymore thought to the pact, even though I'm clearly in it now. We never talked about what was about to transpire on the beach, before we got the call about Morgan, but something changed in that closet. I needed him, and as much more than a friend.

Morgan was sitting in her hospital bed, a hands-free pumping bra strapped around her while those boob shields sucked and sucked at her nipples. It looked fucking painful, and there was just little droplets of milk coming out. This mom thing was for fucking warriors.

"Have you guys decided on a name yet?" I wanted to talk about something positive, to try and pull her out of the sadness that consumed her.

She nodded, the smallest of smiles creeping over her features. "Carina, that's her name."

"Carina." I smiled, "I love it. She is a total Carina."

"She is. I went to see her last night while Jeff was sleeping. Just sat with her for a while, and she actually gripped my pinky." Morgan is glowing, and I can just hear that all-consuming love for her daughter in her voice.

I hand her a half of a sandwich, knowing that she's probably forgotten to eat today but she needs to. "She's a fighter, my niece. The strongest baby in that NICU. The strongest baby ever, really."

"I just want to hold her." Morgan frowns, and I know we're veering back toward despair.

"You will, so soon. Right now, she's getting all of the love from you earthside that she possibly can. She just wanted you to see her extra early." I'm overly gooey these days, something I would usually hate, but actually don't mind if it makes my sister feel better.

"Reese sat with me for a while last night, too. I thank God that he works in there, that we have someone on the inside to help us feel better and tell us the truth. If this had to happen, at least we have him."

I nod, his face in the closet looming at the forefront of my mind. "At least we have him."

"He was talking about you." Morgan looks coy.

"I've been sitting here for twelve hours and you are just now bringing this up?" I huff, going into annoyed sister mode.

Morgan shrugs. "I was trying to figure out if I should actually tell you."

She pauses, and I circle my hand for her to continue. "Anddd?"

"He wants to marry you. He flat out told me." Morgan looks at me, daring me to say the same.

"Well, I guess the word about the pact is out, then."

She turns off the pump, disconnecting and handing me bottles. "I already knew, he knew that I knew."

"Well, marriage definitely isn't something that I'm ready for." I get up, going to the sink to wash the used pump parts.

Sisters can always tell when you're lying. "Stop lying, Erin."

See?

"Reese and I had a nice long talk about exactly how he feels about you, and I told him he should hound you until you give in because you two are meant to be together. Everyone knows it. You know it, even though you're too stubborn and cold to admit it. Just give it up, Er."

I dropped the bottle parts, still facing the sterile hospital sink, too chicken to face her. "I can't just give in that easy. Marriage means something different to me. And so does ... divorce."

Morgan is quiet for a moment. "Is that what this is about? Mom and Dad? That's why you haven't given any guy a chance? Erin ..."

"Don't give me the tone that says you think I'm stupid or overdramatic for thinking that." Now I turn, scowling at her.

She pats the bed, telling me to sit down. "I thought that way for a while too. But after a month or two of grieving and being angry, I realized some things. You may not have seen it, but Mom and Dad were not perfect together. They may have given off that impression, but they avoided a lot of arguments and fights by glossing them over. That doesn't work, not in marriage and not in life. You can't just daydream away the problems ... believe me, they tried and it came back to bite them. Passive aggressive is no way to be in a relationship, and it ultimately ended theirs. No marriage is ever perfect, that's your first mistaken thought. Jeff and I fight all the time. Hell, look at what just happened to us, and he's my fucking rock. It's how you love that matters, not if it's perfect. And Reese Collins, damn, does he love you. Don't walk away from that because you're an idiot who thinks love only exists in a Disney-movie sense."

"Don't call me an idiot, jerk." I shove her shoulder a little bit.

But her advice weighed heavy on my mind. Maybe it was about time I gave up the ice-cold bitch routine and traded it for happiness. After all, Reese was the only boy who could give me butterflies the way he did.

Two days later, I'm tapping away at my desk, reviewing and revising one of the writer's articles, when Katie sits directly next to my keyboard, commandeering my personal space like I don't matter.

"So listen, I was think about your blog." She's almost shouting on the open floor of the newsroom, and I want to strangle her immediately.

Would I go to prison if I stabbed her in the hand with a pencil? She's technically invading my property as she combs through my cup of pens.

"No." I practically bark it, so over-tired and stressed from this week in the hospital.

I'm at my wit's end with my life. Why do I continue to settle for shitty situations, when I can just swallow my fears and go for the shit that I actually want?

My blog is making more money than this place now.

I keep trying to deny that Reese is the man who I'm supposed to be with, and always has been.

"Excuse me? Wouldn't want to go and ruin anything, Erin ..." She's grinning, a snide smile that I want to slap off her face.

She thinks she has me cornered. Thinks I'll bend to something else that she wants just so I can keep my side hustle. Thinks she has me cornered and that I owe her to keep her quiet.

"You know what, Katie, you're a snake." I push back from my desk, standing as my chair rolls into the middle of the floor.

Her piggish nose flares, and she rears back like I've actually slapped her. "I wouldn't do that if I were you, Erin."

I wave my finger dangerously close to her face. "No, don't say another word to me. There are some very choice words I'm actually holding back right now, because I am trying to remain as professional as possible, but you are a brown-noser. You are one of those women who likes to step on other women and laugh while she does it. And I'm sick of it. I'm sick of this whole place."

What I really want to do is tell her to go fuck off, but everyone is already watching my freak-out in the middle of the office and the least I can do for myself is not curse. Katie was the last straw on my camel's back, and she just broke it. After everything with my niece, Reese, trying to hold down two jobs while getting my blog off the ground, I was bone-tired.

I didn't want to be here one single second more. Marching into Mike's office, I tried to take a calming breath. It didn't help much.

He looks up, his gaze landing right on my boobs. Christ. "Mike, I've worked here for almost six years, I've put in my time even when I was overlooked and under-utilized. And today, I'm giving you my notice. Actually, I quit. I won't be working my two weeks. You can mail my last paycheck home. And now that I'm not officially you're employee, I can say this ... you're a pervert who sexually abuses his female employees every single day. And they're all too scared to report you because they need money to live, and you're a pig for preying on that."

And with that, I turn, gathering the few personal effects from my desk as my coworkers look on in shock and amusement, and then march my way out.

My head is held high, and it feels like a baby grand piano has been lifted off my chest. I'm scared out of my fucking mind, but right now, that feels like a good thing.

"I want to be with you."

I may have rushed into this a bit, I realize, as Reese stands at his front door, his hand still on the knob, his jaw hanging open.

After my gallant resignation at the Journal, I rushed right over here, not wanting to press pause on anything in my life anymore. It's amazing how freeing it can be to, in not so many words, tell a bunch of people you hate to go fuck themselves.

"I didn't realize you were coming over. You woke me up." He runs a hand through his cropped curls, his abs on full view and sleep still lingering in the corners of his eyes.

I had to pause before I continued on my mission, because damn, he was gorgeous.

Walking into his apartment, uninvited, while he still stands at the door, I launch into it. "I quit my job today. Just up and quit. And I realized something ... I can't just wait for my life to happen to me. I can't be afraid of every single thing just because I have some preconceived notion about it. I want to be a full-time blogger. I want to be my own boss, and do what I love. And

... I want to be with you. Dating, together, whatever you want to call it."

Reese is still standing at the front door, it half ajar, rubbing his head like I've just smacked him upside it with a frying pan. "You want to get married?"

I shuffle my feet. "I'm not saying anything about the pact right now. But I am saying ... let's be together. No one else. Okay?"

He walks to me, kisses me on the nose. "Well, okay. I was already doing that, I just didn't discuss it with you because you'd freak-out and do that whole ice bitch routine on me. But I'm glad you caught up."

That tight ass walks past me, navy blue boxers giving me a nice full view of it as Reese walks. "Well ... all right."

I feel both giddy and free after all of this confessing and change.

"You want some breakfast?" He stands at the kitchen counter, still half naked.

"It's four p.m," I point out.

"Well, it's like seven a.m. for me, but I'll eat anything. Mac and cheese?" His face lights up.

"I feel like you could be in prison, on death row, and they'd ask you for your last meal request, and you'd ask for Kraft." I chuckle, setting my bag down and slipping my shoes off.

"You know it, babe."

Reese stutters in his actions, noticing what he just called me. It's a romantic endearment, and something he's never called me. It's the first time we're acknowledging that we're dating.

"Babe or peas? Because I feel like everyone in the world is babe. I want to be different." I smooth it over, letting him know by my silent agreement that it's okay for him to regard me in a romantic way.

"You'll always be the peas to my carrots." He grins a *Forrest*

Gump grin, and then goes back to making his macaroni and cheese.

"Do you have any candy? I could use some candy as a reward for quitting my shitty job." I walk over to his pantry, scouring it.

Reese walks up behind me, wrapping his arms around my waist and then leaning down to kiss my neck. It's a strange feeling ... almost like coming home. Why did I deny this for so long?

"I think I got so lost in your admitting you wanted to be with me, and the fact that you woke me from my slumber, that I didn't properly congratulate you. I'm so fucking proud of you, peas. You're already killing it with your blog, it's only going to go up from here. Just remember who supported you first when Carrie Bradshaw calls."

I lean back into him, inhaling his rumpled, just out of bed smell. It was addicting. "Thank you. And I'm also glad that all of those episodes of *Sex and the City* paid off for you."

"I can be your Mr. Big. Also, there are Twizzlers right there."

Was it cheesy that he always kept my favorite candy in his pantry? Maybe, but I kind of loved it.

Half an hour later, we're watching *Jeopardy* on the couch, my leg slung over Reese's and his head leaning on my chest as he lounged.

"Let's just do it." Reese forks a spoonful of macaroni and cheese into his mouth.

I snap off a Twizzler between my teeth. "Do what?"

"Have sex."

He says it so nonchalantly that I almost choke on the piece of candy sliding down my throat.

"Excuse me?" I cough through my shocked question.

"Sex. You know, penis in vagina, orgasms, sweat, two becoming one—"

I hold up a hand, cutting him off. "Yeah, I know what sex is, thanks to eighth grade health class. Which you were in, by the way. As my best friend. You know, a best friend you don't get naked and intimate with."

Reese stands up and scoffs. "Oh, come on, peas. You just showed up at my apartment and practically admitted you're crazy about me. And I've seen your boobs. Sex is a big part of any relationship. If we are going to do the damn thing, we have to see if we have any chemistry between us. Not that the kisses between us didn't prove that."

I hold up a finger, my insides quivering at the thought of getting horizontal with the handsome hunk standing in front of me. Damn him, those kisses were good. And I'd been thinking about what more would feel like for months now.

"First of all, shut up. Second of all, I agreed to be together. Not marry you. That doesn't automatically mean you get the milk. You need to buy the cow. Maybe I won't give it up until we get married." I harrumph at the end of my little speech.

That makes Reese nearly choke. "You just admitted we might get married, so ha!"

I growl. "Not fair, you tricked me."

"I couldn't trick you into anything and you know it. Now, can we have sex?" He flashes me the dimple.

"Way to be blunt." I roll my eyes.

"You love it when I'm blunt. If I tried to carry you into the bedroom, with flower petals and candles over every surface, you'd probably barf in your mouth. So here I am, just doing what you asked me to do. Be transparent, not cheesy. And I'm telling you that I'd very much like to have sex with you."

He had a point.

Having sex with Reese. I guess I hadn't *really* thought about it since he initiated this whole pact thing. I'd contemplated being together, got heated over our kisses, and it might have been a passing blip on the radar. But, actual sex?

And now that he'd said it, it was the only thing I could see. Like a screen set up at the forefront of my brain, I was playing every scenario over and over. Reese on top of me, what his cock would look like, how I would feel …

We were adults. We knew what we were doing. And he was respecting my wishes not to turn this into some Julia Roberts' flick.

"Okay. Let's have sex."

She follows me into the bedroom, both of us going to opposite sides of the bed.

It's one of the only times in our lives that I think I've seen Erin be shy, and I realize she's nervous. Good, because I'm nervous too. I'm not too man enough to deny that. It's fucking terrifying, thinking about having sex with the one woman I've always wanted to do this with.

"So should we ..." Erin trails off, not finishing her questioning, but playing with the hem of her T-shirt.

I realize I'm going to have to walk us through this. Swallowing, I try to put on my best "I got this" face, and walk to her side. Smiling what I hope is a warm expression, I gather her into me, holding her hips and caressing them in my hands.

We've always been about wit and banter, and I'm about to crack a joke to ease the tension, but I realize that what we need right now is the opposite of that. This is a big moment, and it should be treated as such. Even if Erin doesn't want fireflies and getting caught in the rain, I'm going to make this special.

Bending down, I meet her mouth with mine, feeling the give of her lips as I kiss her. I nibble on her full lower lip, and move my left hand to tangle in her blond locks, and angle her head so I can take control as I stroke her tongue with my own. Moving down as my right hand sneaks under her shirt, I lay a trail of open mouth kisses across her neck, collarbone, and shoulder as I pull the button-down she'd been wearing from work.

"Mmm ..." Erin purrs, and I know I've found a sweet spot.

The crook of her neck and shoulder, toward the front, sloping toward her breasts, rather than the back. Noted. I suck on that spot again and am rewarded with a groan. My fingers fumble for the buttons on her shirt, wanting to get her naked. My cock is protesting against the restraint of my boxers, my body still mostly bare from when she woke up pounding on my door.

I finally get to the last button with an exaggerated growl, and Erin is looking at me with those chocolate eyes like she might smack me if I don't hurry up. She reaches for me, her hands raking down my bare back, mine finding the smooth flesh beneath the garment now hanging off her shoulders.

I go straight for her bra, panting at the teenage boy's dream I'm about to live out right now. Every summer since she turned thirteen, I have been tortured by those breasts ... supple and larger than average. The perfect tear drops, more than a handful each. My fingers are aching and greedy, pushing the cups down instead of undoing it around the back like a gentleman. Not that I'd be graceful in that attempt ... men were not given bras to wear for a reason. We'd never be able to get them on or off.

"Gah ..." I have to stop what I'm doing when she slides her hands past my waistband, gripping me.

"Wow ... I always wondered ..." Erin gives me a devilish wink.

"And?" I choke on the words as she jerks me, and if she keeps going I don't think I'll be able to stand upright for much longer.

"I didn't nickname you carrots falsely." She smirks.

I won't lie and say my chest doesn't inflate a little with pride.

I have to move us to the bed, or I'll probably trip over myself while she's cupping my balls and tugging my cock. Pulling her with me, I fall backward, both of us bouncing as I land in my king-sized bed.

Erin giggles, but I silence her with my mouth. I want to go slow, but in my head, I keep thinking this is taking too long. I shove my hands into her bra, rolling her nipples between my fingers.

"Ahh, not like that." She drops her head to my neck. "I don't like too much nipple play. Sorry ..."

I put two fingers under her chin, and made her look up at me. "Don't apologize to me in bed. Ever. Just tell me what you like, what makes you feel good. Yeah?"

She nods, her hair fanning out around us like silky curtains.

I flip her over so that her back hits the bed, and her hand comes out of my boxers. I need to focus on her or my one shot at this will be over way before it started. Working quickly, I get her naked, running my hands up and down each part of her, trying to take snapshots in my mind of her rosy flesh beneath me.

Kissing down her thighs, and biting and sucking until I hear her moan, I end up between them, poised to do my best work. I want her screaming my name so that the neighbors hear it. Preparing myself, and squeezing my ass tight to keep from coming, I taste her for the first time.

And nearly faint. Exactly as sweet as I thought she would be. Somewhere in the universe, fifteen-year-old me is giving me a fist bump.

Erin chuckles from above. "The alphabet trick, really? Who have you been sleeping with and why did they lead you to believe that worked?"

My heart sank and my manhood shriveled up into nothing. I

was screwing this up, when what I should be doing is screwing Erin. Screwing her like a bull in heat.

I looked up, her thighs making parentheses around my face. "What, that doesn't feel good?"

She sits up, giving me a sympathetic smile. Great, just what every guy wants while he's trying to give a girl an orgasm. "Reese ... you don't have to use all of those fancy tricks on me. Just lick my pussy, and rub my clit. Anyone who tells you otherwise is bullshitting you."

I raise my hands up as if to say sorry. "You just tell me what you like. All I want to do is make you feel good."

I head back down there, determined to do better. And I think I do, if her moans tell me anything. I suck and lick, rub and finger. I keep it straightforward, no fancy foreplay, and Erin seems to respond. With each stroke of my mouth or hand, she clenches around me, guttural sounds vibrating through her body. I feast on her like I've never eaten a meal in my life.

"I want you, *now*," Erin moans.

God, yes. This is it. I slide my boxers down as I crawl up the bed, kicking them off my feet as I align myself between Erin's thighs. I gaze into her eyes, the same ones that I've looked into for so many years. Her hair, splayed across my pillow. The way her mouth sucks in air, the nervous anticipation sending goose bumps skittering over her skin.

We both hold our breath as I push into her, my cock twitching with the need for release before I'm even halfway inside. I have to grind my teeth together to gain some composure, I don't want to embarrass myself any further.

"I'm not saying this to pad your ego, but I'm not sure you're going to fit." Erin's smile is teasing, but also riddled with anxiety.

"Does it hurt?" I brush my hand down her cheek.

"It's just ... been a while. And ... you're big. But don't let that go to your head." She slaps my butt.

I jump a little, pushing in farther, and we each groan. "Tell me what I can do to make you feel good."

I wanted to know how she got off. I wanted to know how to have her eyes rolling back in her head.

"You know that spot on my neck?"

I stroked just the smallest bit, and bit back a growl of satisfaction. "Yes."

"Bite it until I tell you I'm coming."

The word off her lips, knowing that she was going to come if I did that, it almost made me come. Lust wrapped around my spine as I fully covered my body with hers, angling my lips to slide over the spot that made her moan. Her legs wrapped around my waist, and I gripped her back, lifting her shoulders with my hands to get an angle that had me quivering as I drove into her.

And the whole time, I was sucking on her neck, probably tattooing the imprint of my lips on it. Erin was sobbing with pleasure as I pounded, alternating from fast to slow, deep to shallow strokes. I was losing my damn mind, exerting myself emotional and physically to the brink of madness.

"I'm going to—" Erin couldn't even finish the thought before she was wailing, clawing at my back.

My lips stayed pressed to that spot on her neck as I reached the edge, gasping into blackness as I came, shooting hot and forceful inside her.

There had never been anything more natural than this. I was home, and she'd always been the place I was meant to end up in.

28

Having lived in my apartment for almost five years, I know the sounds and goings-on of the outside world at every time of day.

Which is why I bolt awake when church bells that I do not recognize as part of my neighborhood begin chiming. I sit up like I've just pulled myself out of a dream where rabid dogs are chasing me, or I get a really bad haircut.

Reese's gray sheets pool around me, more like T-shirt material instead of the silky linens I have on my bed. They're not bad, just different.

Which is kind of how my new relationship status with Reese is. It's not bad, it's just different. And by bad, I mean holy cow, that sex blew my mind. After we both stopped trying so hard, or trying to respect the other's feelings. Or doing that stupid shit that men and women do to come off sexy without actually feeling satisfied during sex. Yeah, we put all of that aside, and my world literally shook. I didn't know it could do that.

No man had ever actually asked me how I wanted it. But then again, I'd never been comfortable enough to express my desires to another man. I felt comfortable with Reese, and the weirdness of being with him in a sexual way faded quickly when I'd seen how big his cock was. I mean, damn, had I been missing out for all of these years. I may not have a penchant for romance and heart-eyes, but I could appreciate a beautiful penis. And Reese? He had a beautiful penis.

The only thing I have on are my underwear, and I realized I came over here with nothing. Not even a toothbrush, although Reese didn't seem to mind my breath when he was drilling me from behind for the second time last night.

It's not like I've never worn my best friend's clothes before. Hell, my favorite hangout T-shirt was one of his Mathletes shirts from high school. Speaking of Reese, where was he?

Besides the foreign sounds from outside his apartment, I didn't hear a shower or the microwave. Or the TV on the *Today Show*, Reese's favorite morning show. He is a big Al Roker fan.

Glancing over at his spot on the bed, I see a piece of paper folded on his pillow. Picking it up, I can't deny that I let out a girly sigh when I read it.

Peas,

This is my first love note to you. Forget about all of those other notes I sent you in high school that complained about being in class or that my parents took the car away from me again. This is the real deal.

Last night was incredible. You look absolutely stunning as I write this, watching you sleep. And don't roll your eyes at that, it's not creepy. You're gorgeous and lying in my bed naked, I couldn't not stare. In fact, never leave my bed.

I had to go to the hospital for an early morning shift, but I left coffee in the pot. Stay awhile. Relax, you deserve it. Or, like I know you will because you can't sit still, use my computer to start planning how Shoes and the City is going to take over the blogging world. I am so proud of you. Text me when you wake up.

Forever yours,
Carrots

It was corny, but so typical Reese that I had to smile. And somewhere deep down, that iceberg that encased my heart melted a little more. Funny how he had begun to chip and sink it since he moved back to Philly.

Getting up, I stroll to his dresser, looking for a soft, long T-shirt to putz around in. When I found one, a Dallas Mavericks T-shirt that I bet he wouldn't show to his Seventy-Sixer fan friends, I throw it on and go to the kitchen.

Reese, again, knows me too well. He left me a full pot of coffee, knowing that I need at least three cups to be a fully-functioning human in the morning.

I take my mug to the couch, along with Reese's laptop, taking full advantage of his offer. No reason to rush around and get out of here, another perk of having a no pants sleepover with your best friend. I'd spent so much time in Reese's various spaces that I did not feel at all compelled to pull my shoes on in the middle of the night and disappear before the sun came up. No matter what happened between us now, we were always going to be friends in some sense of the word.

Hopefully, it was not just friends. Hopefully, it was now ... lovers. Bleh, I hated that word. Boyfriend and girlfriend? It sounded too mundane, didn't encompass the largeness of what we shared.

Firing up the laptop, I logged into my Gmail, and opened my blog site to edit mode so that I could view analytics and layout. I had two new partnership offers, one with a shoe company and the other with a sunglass company that was all over Instagram, it was like the syphilis of social media.

I'd made a promise to myself when I first started my blog and brand that I wasn't going to do this simply to make money. I was really going to back products and fashion that I loved, both expensive and for the everyday woman. At the beginning, I'd kind of deviated from this when I began to get offers from every Insta-hungry brand who would pay anyone to rep their stuff. But my page began to get bogged down in shit that I didn't even particularly like, and I professionally parted ways with almost all of those companies.

It might not garner me as much money, but slowly I'd built relationships with brands that I actually wanted to be involved with. So this sunglass company was an absolute no, but the shoe company was interesting. A startup brand from Brooklyn, they had a lot of camel-colored slide sandals, and some suede. It said that their faux leather and materials were locally sourced, and the backstory of the owner of the company was interesting.

Responding that I'd be interested in receiving and reviewing a couple of pairs, I then combed through my social media for possible partnerships. Because building a brand wasn't about sitting idly by and waiting for things to fall in your lap. It was about sending hundreds, thousands, of PR emails promoting yourself and your blog. However awkward it felt to contact a stranger and ask them to help you out, that's essentially what you had to do. You could do it in a friendly and cordial way, but in the end, you had to do it.

And after a while, and about five hours sitting at the computer working, I just decided to stay at Reese's. I made dinner for him, a simple spaghetti and frozen meatballs was about all I could whip up. But I did it. And I waited for him to get home.

Then I stayed the next day, when he had a day off. And the next morning, when he didn't have to go in until his night shift.

We really brushed up on our "lovers" skills. I still detested the word, but for what went down between us the next two days … that was an accurate term.

Because we were now a couple, we were in that stage where we wanted everyone else around us to also be a couple.

Why this unconscious setting up thing always happened, I wasn't sure. Maybe it was because we were having great sex, and wanted our friends to be having great sex, too. With each other. Which, if you thought about it, was almost always a bad idea. These kinds of setups always ended in bitterness, and the friend talking shit about the other friend. And then your girlfriend was constantly bitching that your guy friend screwed her friend over ...

Fuck. Was I creating a mess waiting to happen?

"Why are we setting two people up? We can barely function as a couple ourselves. Hell, it took almost twenty years for us to get together, I don't think we have any business playing cupid." Erin squeezes my hand, our fingers intertwined.

She was always reading my mind.

I shrug. "Maybe not, but Preston is single as fuck and never leaves the hospital. He needs to branch out. And you said Jill was ecstatic at the prospect of meeting a hot doctor, so ..."

Erin raises an eyebrow at me. "You never introduced me to any hot doctors."

"That's because this hot nurse was keeping you all to himself." I hug and shake her while using some self-deprecating humor toward myself.

Erin giggles and rolls her eyes. "God, that sounds so much sexier."

Jill walked up at that moment, meeting us outside the Thai restaurant we'd all agreed on. I'd met her a few times while we were all in college, and I'd always liked Erin's close friend. Mostly because Erin didn't have a lot of other friends, and if she did, they were cool. Like me.

"I did not think I'd ever see the day." Jill smiles, pointing to our interlaced hands.

I can feel Erin blush at the public display of embarrassment, something I insisted on. So instead of holding our conjoined hands up like I just won a prized boxing fight, I just grin.

"I finally got her to fall in love with me."

I feel Erin bristle, because we have not said that four letter word in this context yet. But I've figured out, over the last few months, that if I don't drag her along, she'll never be ready for any of it.

"And I'm damn glad about that. The Ice Queen has a king ... I'm so happy for you guys." Jill grabs us in a tight group hug.

"Can we stop all of this touching? You're both freaking me out," Erin snips at us, annoyed.

Jill ignores her. "I'm just so happy for you guys. Okay, now prepare me for the hot doctor."

She backs up, smooths down her dress, and looks at me like I am the Washington Press Secretary giving her a debrief. "Um ... well, I won't lie. He's not the most social of guys, but he is nice and loves his job."

Jill blinks, and Erin cuts in. "Not the most social of guys ... what does that mean?"

I try to come up with something that sounds positive. "He uh ... doesn't really leave the hospital. Doesn't have the best bedside manner but is a genius when it comes to the field of medicine. Isn't interested in making friends."

Well, I couldn't do it.

Jill throws her hands up. "Great! You're setting me up with Scrooge!"

Erin throws me a scowl and then pats Jill's back. "Who knows, maybe he just doesn't like Reese that much so he's trying to blow him off."

"Hey! Preston likes me, we've gotten beers together."

My girl shakes her head. "You're digging yourself deeper, carrots. Let's go get our table, your friend is late."

Ten minutes later, Preston hurries into the restaurant. At least he's not wearing scrubs, but his jeans and polo are a little underdressed for this Thai place. Whatever, I'm surprised he didn't cancel. Poor guy had sounded so freaked out when I suggested this double date.

"Hi, sorry I'm late. Emergency at the hospital." He nods at me.

"Yeah, I'm sure." My voice is all sarcasm, because he was probably contemplating whether he should actually come or not.

Preston sits down across from Jill, and I can tell he thought she was hot. His mouth practically hung open, he was staring at her lips, and for a guy whose hands were always steady, they were most definitely fidgeting.

Shit, he probably has no game, and I was sending him into the shark's tank. Jill was whip-smart and had the confidence to back it up. I hope she went easy on him.

"Nice to meet you, Preston, I'm Erin. Reese is clearly too rude to introduce me, but I'll just ignore him then." Erin held her hand out for Preston to shake across the table.

He took it unsurely. "Uh, nice to meet you. But for the record, I don't think Reese is rude. He's extremely competent as a nurse, and always has patience for anyone who comes into the NICU."

Erin raises a brow at me. "Wow, how much did you pay him?"

I kiss her cheek, annoying her with the PDA. "I didn't, he's just that nice. And that literal."

"You must be Jill, it's very nice to meet you." Preston focuses fully on Erin's friend, and I can see instantly that she's smitten with the hot doctor.

Erin and I exchange a glance where we sit across from each other, and I do an internal fist pump in celebration for my awesome pairing.

We order a round of drinks and appetizers, and Jill launches into a story about what happened on her latest flight.

"So I was going to see a client out in Texas, the flight was about four hours. Of course, the woman next to me takes off her shoes twenty minutes into the flight, no socks."

Preston intervenes. "That's highly unsanitary. Planes contain some of the highest germ counts you could ever encounter."

Jill reaches for his hand, shaking it. "Thank you, right?! So gross."

Preston looks at their joined hands and I swear, he blushes. For being such an introverted nerd, he definitely has feelings for the obnoxious but lovable extrovert sitting across from him.

"So then, like two hours into this flight, I hear her rustling around in her bag. And out she pulls ... a bag of garlic, parmesan fries! On the plane! They were chilling in her bag for likes two hours, probably so soggy, and she's stinking up the whole flight with them. People are so weird!"

We're all laughing, with Erin clutching her stomach she's cracking up so much.

"This one time, I was at medical conference, and I was in the bathroom during a break, and two doctors walked out after relieving themselves, without even washing their hands!" Preston stretches his hands out as if to demonstrate how gross their hands were.

I'm surprised he even told a story, because he's usually not one to go out of his comfort zone and actively make conversation.

"Ew, that is gross! I always wonder if doctors or like, fast food workers actually wash their hands. You know those signs in the bathroom? Do they ever abide by them?" Jill and Preston begin a side conversation about disgusting habits, and I smile at Erin.

"Told you so," I whisper, under my breath.

She shrugs, relenting. "Who knew?"

After dinner, Erin and I head out to the sidewalk, with Preston and Jill trailing behind, still deep in conversation.

"Would you like to go get a drink with me?" Preston asks her, and my jaw almost hits the floor.

He has to be really smitten with her to not want to head straight back to the hospital.

"Sure." Jill blushes. "See you later guys."

We all play the goodbye game, and then they're off, single and ready to mingle.

"Wow, we are really good matchmakers. I mean, who would have known those two would work. I guess Jill found someone who doesn't mind her rambling. Preston is nice. Kind of weird, but nice. Thanks for suggesting it."

Erin pushes up on her toes and kisses me on the street, right there on the Philadelphia street. We walk back to my apartment with our arms linked around each other's backs, and I bask in that new romance bliss.

After two weeks of spending almost every day together —hey, a woman who ran her own business could work from anywhere, which was working for me— Erin and I knew we would have to tell our mothers.

If they found out that we were finally seeing each other by mistake, or knew we'd been hiding it for already as long as we had been, there would be some serious mom guilt thrown upon us.

That's how we ended up at my parent's front door, our hands laced together while I held a box of Italian cookies from my mom's favorite bakery in my other hand.

Knocking, I looked over at Erin, who looked like she was sweating bullets. "You ready for this?"

She shrugged and looked nervous. "I guess we were going to have to tell them sooner or later. But, I just don't think I'm ready for all of the high-pitched screaming."

Before I can assure her for the fiftieth time, the other forty-nine happened in the car, my mom opens the door.

"Oh, sweetheart, I'm so glad you came, I missed you ... oh,

Erin! I didn't realize you were coming too! I'm so happy you're here—"

Mom rambles for a little and we let her, all standing at the door, until she realizes that we're holding hands. And not letting go. We just let her look at them until she lets out that high-pitched scream that Erin was afraid of.

"Stop. Stop it right now, Reese Maximus. Is this some sort of joke? Is this real? If this is real, I am going to sob. Don't stop me if it is."

And right there, she starts to cry actual tears of joy. I look at Erin and roll my eyes, and she shoots me an "I told you so" look. Mom does a giddy little jump and then rushes Erin, sweeping her into a big hug on my childhood front steps.

"Ah! I have been waiting for this day for such a long time. I honestly didn't know if it would come, but how happy I am that it did! I am going to have a daughter. The daughter I always thought would be my daughter! Oh my gosh, Erin, I am so happy." Mom is literally crying on her shoulder.

Erin is shooting me a look as if to say help me, and I pat Mom on the back. "All right, all right, calm down. Why don't we go in and have some coffee? I brought your favorite cookies."

Mom shoots up, looking like a lightbulb that just got an idea. "I have to tell your father. *Chris!*"

She ran into the house, leaving us to let ourselves in while she scuttled around for Dad. I inhaled the air of my parent's house ... it was always the same. Peppermint from the ever-growing bush my mom kept in the backyard to make tea from. The scent of my dad's leather shoes that he still polished weekly. And French vanilla, my mom's favorite candle that I bought her for Mother's Day each year.

Erin and I walk into the kitchen, a place we spent many an hour while growing up. Whether it was snacks after school, lemonade in the summer after running around like maniacs, or late night munching after we'd gone to a high school party ... I had so many memories with her in this kitchen.

"Remember the time that we tried to make nachos after that summer party between sophomore and junior year of college?" Erin chuckles.

"Yeah and the woman who doesn't know how to cook forgot to put cheese on them before putting them in the microwave. They just turned out to be really hot, soft chips," I tease her.

"Well, at least you knew my résumé before you started dating me. Cooking is a definite shortcoming."

"It's okay, most of my meals are eaten in the hospital anyhow, and I never cared that you hate to cook. Although, I think I could find some nice things to do with ice cream and you. Or whipped cream and you. Or chocolate syrup and you." I wink at her, careful to show my dimple as well.

Erin blushes and swats at me. "Shut up, your parents are going to hear you."

Just as she says it, my parents walk into the kitchen. Dad shakes my hand and hugs Erin. "Your mom is making a fuss that you two are dating. Wasn't this a thing that's been going on a long time?"

My father was always a great dad, even if he missed some of the more minute details. "Uh, no, Dad, we've just been really good friends up until now. But yes, we are dating *now*."

Mom squeals again. "Oh my, does Barbara know yet? Let me get her over here!"

Erin places a hand on my mom's and shakes her head. "I know you're excited and we are too. But ... just let me tell her on my own, okay?"

We'd discussed this when we talked about coming home to tell my parents. Barbara was ... fragile. Even five years after the divorce, you couldn't announce a wedding or a baby around her without careful consideration of how the discussion would go down. I remember she didn't get out of bed for a week after Morgan had announced her engagement. She was so wrapped up in her failure of marriage that she couldn't be happy for her own daughter.

"Probably for the best, dear." Mom pats Erin's hand and looks at her like she invented sliced bread. "Chris, aren't they just the most magnificent thing you've ever seen? When do I get a grandbaby?"

Erin practically chokes on the glass of iced tea Dad had set down in front of her, and I have to laugh. "Mom, give us a hot second."

She pouts, taking a pound cake out of that glass thing that always sat on the counter. "I've waited thirty years for this moment, and you two took long enough."

"Leave them be, honey. The kids are happy, can we settle with that for now?" My dad, always the voice of reason, rubbed her shoulders.

"Fine, but I want weekly dinner. We haven't seen you enough since you've been back, and now that Morgan has the baby, I bet you'll all be in the suburbs more."

Erin smiles at her, and I remember how close they are. She's practically her second mother, and I realize that it's never felt right introducing other women to my parents because it was always meant to be Erin.

"You've got yourself a deal. Just don't make me pinky promise, because that may take a while to come to fruition."

And then Erin looks at me and winks.

Can she even imagine how crazy I am about her?

Now that I no longer had a day job, just a twenty-four seven, hustle-my-ass-off job, I was free to do things in the middle of the day.

Like go to the dentist, or get my moles checked ... two things that working people definitely could not do since those places only stayed open until five or six. When I had my job at the Journal, I don't think I went to the dentist for a year. That's gross ... but who has time to take off work to get their teeth cleaned? Certainly not me.

One of the other things I could now do was visit Carina any hour of the day ... which I did, pretty much every day at three.

I would work on the blog, do photo shoots, design marketing campaigns, and try on samples I'd been sent in the morning, all before about noon. And then I'd head to Morgan's, where she was just getting back from a six hour shift sitting in the NICU with Carina. I'd bring her lunch and eat there, then head over to see my niece for an hour each day.

My family were practically regulars now at CHOP. The security guards knew our names, and Mom's famous cobbler. The doctors all knew who we were, and although I technically wasn't allowed to visit my niece by myself, Reese helped make an exception for us. Good thing I was dating someone who could give us NICU perks.

Jesus, how many times did you hear that in your life? Remind me next time to date someone who can get me concert tickets for free, or maybe a ride on a private plane. For now, this was working out perfectly.

Although, the other benefits with Reese were turning out to be spectacular ...

Though things with my mother were not. She had a bit of a freak-out when I told her that we were dating. I'd gone to her house for lunch last week, and dropped the news on her. Typically, she was a bit of a nervous person, anxiety riddled her, but after the divorce it amplified by a hundred.

She'd been gobsmacked, told me I was reckless, asked how I could throw away a good friendship for something as unstable as love? It made me doubt everything, and even though she was going through her own shit, I'd run to my sister to talk me down off a ledge. Morgan was obviously pissed at our mother for never being able to see past her own insecurities. She'd told me to take whatever she said with a grain of salt, and that we weren't going to change her so just trust my own gut instinct and be happy.

I scrubbed my fingernails with the red sanitizing soap they have on the surgical sinks in the entrance room of the NICU, and donned a yellow scrub jacket that covered practically my entire body.

Walking in, there are two other sets of parents sitting across the room in their individual spaces, their babies in either cribs or incubators. Carina's bassinet, she's been downgraded from the enclosed plastic box, sits in the corner in a different row, and I quietly make my way there. I nod to one of the female nurses I recognize, and Preston is speaking to another family halfway across the room, by the nurse's desk.

Reese is nowhere to be seen, but I didn't come here for him, just to spend some time with my girl. I picture her as I walk, black hair, pale creamy skin, an impossibly pink mouth, she was a perfect mixture of Jeff and Morgan. They said that all babies were born with dark blue eyes, but the couple of times I'd actually caught her awake, they were bright green, the exact color of my sister's eyes.

When I finally reach her bassinet, I stop dead in my tracks, as if I've seen a ghost.

Because I am. I'm staring right at a ghost, holding my baby niece.

"What the fuck are you doing here?" My voice is too loud, and someone in the row of bassinets over shushes me.

Sitting in front of me, like a deer caught in headlights, is a man I have barely seen over the last five years. Holding my niece, who is attached to wires and machines coming out of the wall.

My father, the man who left his family behind, is sitting there cradling his granddaughter like he's been any part of this family for the past five years.

"Erin ..." He looks like he wants to get up, to hug me, to say something, but Carina is in his arms.

He's graying, more than he was the last time I saw him two years ago. Still the picture of my face, I always did look more like him than mom. It rattles me at times when I look at my own reflection in the mirror. He still has that scar above his left eyebrow from the time he hit his head on the roof cleaning out the gutters. And he's looking at the baby like this isn't the first time he's seen her. Which obviously makes me seethe with anger. Has Morgan been allowing him to come see her? We were going to have words about this.

"No. Why are you here?" I don't want to hear any of his bullshit.

It has taken me five years to even set my rage toward him to simmer ... before it had been on full blast, high heat. The way he left his wife, my mother, telling her that he didn't love her anymore ... it was a dismantling of our family. Thirty years of marriage down the drain, all because he couldn't stay invested.

"She is my granddaughter. I have the right to know her. I'm so sorry, so sorry. I've been trying to tell you for so long now ..." My father rocks Carina as she begins to squirm.

"I don't want to hear it. You should say you're sorry to my mother," I rage whisper.

His eyes grow cold. "What happened between your mother and I was my fault, I've admitted that many times. But that is between us, and frankly, Erin, you've never been fully clued in to what's going on. I'm glad you haven't, because you grew up with a childhood that seemed blissfully perfect. That's what I hope for all children, what I hope for Carina. But as an adult, you need to grow up. Things are not always as they seem, and we've lost a lot of time because of your inability to realize that. I won't let it happen to my granddaughter and me."

The old man doesn't seem like he's going anywhere. I'm either going to stay here, or risk leaving and not having my day with Carina. As much as I love her, I don't think I can sit across from him and make small talk about the weather. Plus, I'm too fired up to have calming energy around my niece, who needs to heal.

What I do need is to find the two people who have known that he's been coming to visit and haven't told me.

For the second time in a matter of months, Erin shows up, pounding at my door in the middle of the day when I should be sleeping.

I open it, expecting her to jump my bones or say that she forgot I'd been on night shift. But instead, she stomps past me, yelling words that my sleepy brain only half comprehends.

"You knew he was visiting! And you didn't tell me! How dare you, Reese Collins!" She slaps my bare chest and then storms away again.

"Huh?" I scratch my head, the sting of her slap reverberating through my skin.

"And Morgan, Jesus, how could she?! He's a liar and a ruiner of lives ... and she let him around her daughter!" She throws her hands up, incensed.

"What are you talking about?" I have to pause in the middle of my sentence to yawn.

She's in heavier makeup than usual, and her hair is all curled and long ... she must have done a photo shoot this morning and she smells delicious. Like spring flowers and strawberries. Angry Erin is fucking sexy, and my boxers tent a little at her furious expression.

She must notice it, because her brown eyes turn black and her expression could kill me if it actually wanted to. "Don't even think about it."

Her tone could melt flesh. I touch my face, checking if she's done it to mine. "Peas, I have no idea what's going on."

"My father, that's what." She crosses her arm and taps her foot in the middle of my kitchen.

Shit. I forgot to tell her when I'd seen him for the first time visiting last week. Well, maybe I'd just avoided the subject. What she didn't know wouldn't hurt her, and Morgan and I had agreed that maybe we should allow David to get to know Carina without the stress of having to answer to Erin for a while. I had never said this to my best friend, but he deserved the chance to be a part of their family.

Erin thought about love and trust in such one dimensional ways, when in reality, those two things were made up of so many elements.

"Peas, please sit down and listen to me." I grab a T-shirt that I had discarded over the back of my couch and pull it on.

Reluctantly, Erin sits down on the couch, eyes still full of piss and vinegar. "You lied to me."

I roll my eyes and sit next to her. "Stop that, we're not playing that game. We're too old, and you're not mad at me. You're not mad at any of us really. You're just salty over this situation, and I know that because we're best friends and have been for decades. I'm sorry you had to find out like that, but don't become a drama queen on me. You aren't one, but if you need to, you can claw at me and we can have angry sex."

Erin scowls deeper at me. "Nice try. Maybe you're right, but God, he's such an asshole. Sitting there, holding Carina, acting like nothing even happened."

"I'm sure he wasn't acting like that ..." I raised an eyebrow at her.

She pouted, sticking out her bottom lip. "Why are you not on my side? Stop playing devil's advocate."

"I'm always on your side, except for the issues that I think you're wrong about and will end up regretting."

Erin continues like I haven't even spoken. "He has no right to be in our lives. Leaving our mother like that. He never even loved her. How can you love someone when you do something like that to them?"

I sigh, knowing this might cause World War III. "I'm going to say something now and you're going to let me finish, even if your blood is boiling by the end. Okay?"

Crossing her arms over her chest, she nods. "Fine."

Breathing, I compose myself. Because no one ever wants to tell someone that they love deeply that they're wrong. And that most of their views are wrong. But, I try to tell myself it's coming from a good place.

"Because your view on love isn't realistic, not in the way you think. I'm sorry, but it's true. You think that love doesn't exist, that romance is dead and falling for someone is only for fools. But you're wrong. Deep down, you know that's wrong. The reason you're so fucking scared is because you know the truth. And the truth of it is, you think love is supposed to be perfect. This swirling ball of brilliant brightness that eclipses every bad thing. That conquers fears and solves war. But it's not. Love is so far from perfect. Love means standing by someone's side even when they're an asshole. Even when one of you gets sick, terminally so. Love means saying you're sorry when you argue about directions and then realize the other person was looking at the map right all along. It doesn't mean sunshine and rainbows twenty-four seven. So you don't have to believe in love, not in the form of perfection you think it exists as. But, you *do* have to believe that loving the right person means you'll also hate them sometimes, and that's okay."

Erin blinks at me as if I've just dropped a truth bomb so explosive on her, she is shell-shocked.

I continue. "And clearly, your mom and dad didn't have the love that can outlast something huge, like a zombie apocalypse. I know that hurts when I say it, but someone has to. Morgan has grasped that, she's been seeing him for years without discussing it with you. We all walk on tiptoes around you when it comes to your father, but we can't do that any longer. He's a good guy, the same Dad that you grew up with. That took us to Six Flags and baseball games and grilled dozens and dozens of clams for your birthday every year because he knew that you loved them. Your mother, and I love her but it's true, has played a miserable spinster victim since they split. She did the one thing you're not supposed to as a parent if you divorce; she poisoned the kids. I think it's about time you sit down and talk to your dad, get past this. If you don't ... you'll regret it, I'm telling you, you will."

I take hold of her hands, and a tear leaks down her cheek. "I just don't know how not to be so angry with him."

Kissing her cheek, I nod into the tear and wipe it away with my own face. "It won't be easy, but this much fury is not good for you. Especially my little peas."

"I hate you for knowing me so well. For picking the other side."

I cradle her into me. "Like I said, I'm always on your side."

There is a pause, where Erin just breathes in my shirt and I stroke her hair. I could tell her right now that I love her, that I've always been in love with her.

But the moment is not right. She's too upset, coming down off of her tirade. Or maybe I'm just too chicken.

Either way, I don't say those three little words for what seems like the hundredth missed opportunity in my life.

ERIN

My hips thrusted wildly, the bones so spent but a subconscious tic inside of me would not let me stop until I reached it.

Orgasm.

Coming.

Climax.

I rode Reese like my life depended on it, frantically, deranged. Out of my mouth came noises that I couldn't even comprehend, and my whole body was shaking like I was detoxing from the hardest of drugs. I was teetering, my nails imbedded into Reese's chest, his words spurring me on.

"Come on, Erin, come for me. Let me see that beautiful face I'm waiting for. Ride me, baby, make yourself come."

Each time he said the word come, I shuddered. I was so close to the brink of pleasure, and I needed to reach it. Stretching my thighs even farther apart as I straddled him, I ground down, my clit making contact with his groin.

"Oh my God!" I cried, rubbing myself on him that way twice before my orgasm stole over all of my limbs.

For a couple of mind-numbing seconds, the world disappears, and it's just sensation. My nerves fraying. Sensations only.

And then I'm sucked back to earth as if someone pulled the drain out, and I collapse onto Reese's chest, spent.

"God, you're fucking hot," he growls.

I'm used to hearing him in sex mode now, but the rawness of his voice still rattles me. Deep and tender, like cool silk or velvety coffee poured over ice.

I have to lean back up, because he's taken over, and I need to see him.

Reese is glorious, his eyes tilted up to the ceiling like he's trying to pray that he won't pass out. His face is tensed in concentration as his wrists and hands slam me down on top of him, tingles from my own orgasm shooting out to my extremities, keeping my climax alive and buzzing through my body. His chest is cut but not buff, his arms lean but not bulky. He's got the build of a swimmer, tall, and lean with muscles that aren't obvious.

A roar rips from his throat, almost imitating an actual lion's, when he comes. His hips sway and jut up into me, and I fear I may split open if he goes any deeper.

After, I lie on his sweat-slicked chest, my own sweat mixing with his and creating a gross concoction if you actually thought about it.

"We're getting pretty good at that." Reese sighs into my knotted mane.

"Practice makes perfect, as they say." I trace patterns in the smattering of hair on his chest.

"You going to get off?" He makes a move like he's going to roll over.

But I keep us in place. "I thought I just did."

"Har, har, very funny. But come on, I have a cramp in my ass."

He turns us, stretching his leg once we become dislodged and shaking it to relieve the cramp. We lie intertwined, speaking without words, in that post-sex way that always seems to happen. Soft grunts, sighs, fingertips lightly tickling backs ... it's a language unto its own.

After a couple of minutes, I get up to pee, no one wants a urinary tract infection because they were lazy after sex. Trust me, I've gotten one, it's not pretty.

When I get back in my bed, sliding under the sheets and comforters seeking Reese's arms, his eyes are drifting.

I pinch his nipple, startling him. "Wake up, it's only nine p.m."

He tickles me violently, and I shake him off. "I have constant jet lag, remember? I'm a nurse. Also, we're almost thirty. We're old, we should be in bed by nine."

"I refuse. I'm going to pull all-nighters even when I'm seventy."

"I'd like to see you try." He kisses me on the nose.

A couple more minutes of silence go by, and I reach over to turn the light on so that we don't conk out. I scroll through my feeds for a bit, getting lost in the perfectly pictured flowers, outfits and couples shots.

"How come we never talked about the New Year's kiss? Or the one on your twenty-first birthday?" Reese looks at me, the lamp light all too bright now for the question he's asking.

I squirm and put my phone down, suddenly uncomfortable. "I don't know, it's not like you brought them up either."

"That's because I knew you weren't ready to talk about it. To go there. And I initiated both ... you had to have known I always secretly wanted more."

I sit up a little, because this a revelation to me. "Wait, what?"

Reese blows out a breath and scoots up my headboard, leaning against it and crossing his arms over his naked abs. "I've had a crush on you since the moment we met, peas. I've always thought you were the most beautiful thing I've ever seen. And then I got to be your friend, and learn how funny and amazing you are. Those two times ... I was trying to tell you without telling you, how I felt. Both of those mornings after, I was waiting for you to realize that, or at least say something. And when you didn't ... I just left it alone. Thought you didn't want me in that way. I didn't want to ruin our friendship."

Realization blossoms inside my chest, and I slap my forehead. "I have been the biggest idiot. Honestly, Reese, I never knew. I thought they were just drunken hookups, that I was the closest female to you and you acted on a horny impulse. If you wanted me to know about those feelings, you should have just told me."

He levels with me. "And how would you have responded? We both know you would have freaked-out. It was never the right timing."

I look down at my hands. "You're probably right. But I was stupid then, and even after that, my views on love and relationships shifted. And then they shifted again. Because the timing is right now. And the person I'm with, you, shifted them. We never talked about those kisses because it would have sunk us. But we're talking about them now, and hell, I think we're getting better at them. Like you said."

I wink at Reese, and he touches me once more. This time, his hands splay on my open thighs, where I sit cross-legged on the bed.

"You really are the most beautiful thing I've ever seen." He rubs his hands up and down my skin, stoking the flames once more.

"Don't go getting all soft on me, carrots." I reach below the sheet that covers his waist, grazing his half-hard cock.

"Who you calling soft?" He gyrates his hips into my hand,

and is hard in another millisecond.

I think I'm going to be pulling an all-nighter.

"No wonder this baby is thriving, you give her more attention than three nurses combined."

Preston walks over to where I sit in the rocking chair by Carina's bassinet, holding her and talking to her as she watches me. In the past few weeks, she's gained four pounds, is eating from a bottle, having regular bowel movements (a great, if not disgusting, sign), and has begun to look around when you talk to her. She's almost ready to go home, and if it means me working two extra shifts a week to get her there, I'll do it.

"I always think that human contact really helps them. And I may be a bit biased toward her." I let her grab onto my finger, her grip strong and reassuring.

"It's a proven scientific fact, so yes, I'll agree." He nods.

"How is your shift going?" I give Carina a kiss, something I'm probably not allowed to do but I know this little one, and then set her down in her crib for a nap.

"Not too bad, I won't say quiet because we know the jinx that puts on things." Preston shrugs.

"You may have just jinxed us just with that sentence." I give him a pointed look. It's like saying Macbeth in a theater.

We walk to the front desk of the NICU, a couple of other nurses nodding at us as we pass. It's an odd time of day, around eight p.m. Either the parents with babies here have left for the night, or won't be in until after dinner if they have other kids at home. Sometimes, we'll have the odd visitor, but this is usually the downtime of this unit.

I log Carina's stats, and then the stats of my other baby I've been watching this shift. We each have two a shift, who are on relatively different schedules. All of their feedings, poops and sleeps are logged and accounted for, so that the doctors can make the best diagnosis and treatment if something were to happen.

"So, I went out with Jill again yesterday." Preston shuffles his feet, trying to casually drop his dating life into conversation.

But we're good friends now, having worked together for more than a couple of months, and I know he wouldn't bring up something personal unless he wanted to talk about it.

"I'm happy you did, man. How was it? She's a great girl."

He nods. "She's amazing. Smart and funny, and she knows how to keep the conversation going. If you couldn't tell, I'm probably not the greatest social dater."

I smirk. "Nah, I couldn't tell."

To his credit, Preston gets my sarcasm for once, and even rolls his eyes. I almost fall off my chair. "I really like her, I just ... she's going to tire of me eventually."

His face falls, and I clap a hand on his shoulder, squeezing in that manly way that we men do. "Don't say that, man. I know Jill, and she does not stay with someone if she's not interested. Trust me, I saw her on that first date, she's interested."

"She won't be for long. I ... I can already sense myself doing the same old thing." He looks so little like the confident doctor that I'm used to.

I have a feeling this is going to drudge up some baggage. "What is that?"

Preston sighs, looking around to make sure that no one is listening to us. The other five nurses on this shift, plus the number of administrative personnel and doctors, are either rounding, doing notes by a bassinet, or in their offices.

"I haven't ... you know ... done it. I haven't in a really long time." He looks so embarrassed, his tan skin turning a deep shade of red.

I squirm, both interested but not sure if I should be the one having this conversation with him. "How long is a really long time?"

"Remember how I told you about my high school sweetheart?" He picks up a pen from the desk and begins to tap it rhythmically on the Formica counter.

I nearly choked on my own spit, and I have to physically clap my chest a couple of times to clear my throat. "I'm sorry ... you were what, eighteen? You're telling me you haven't had sex in ten years?"

He shushes me. "Keep it down. I don't need that advertised in here."

I blink. "Sorry ... I just, I'm not even sure I know how that's possible. You're a goddamn monk, man."

Preston grimaces. "It's possible. I've gotten very acquainted with myself."

"I can imagine. Jesus, man, why?" My mind is boggled.

I can't imagine not having sex for a month, less a year. But ten years? I would go insane. They'd have to literally check me into the psych floor.

Preston looks around again, but no one is paying any attention to us. "Ever since what happened, you know ... getting my girlfriend pregnant. Well, she was the first girl I ever slept with. And look how that turned out. My brain, it just won't let me. I've come close a couple of times, and I ... just can't. Something is mentally blocking me. I've done studies on it, tried to diagnose myself and treat it. But nothing works. And believe me, I know the thing still works. Just not around pretty women."

I blow out a breath. "Jeez, I'm sorry. Maybe you could go see a therapist? Talk it out with someone?"

He waves me off. "I don't believe in that feelings crap. Medicine should be able to fix it."

I wasn't going to get into that argument with him. I didn't see it that way, but he was so straight-laced and set in his opinions that I was tired just thinking about debating with him.

"Well, man ... don't count yourself out. You never know. Maybe it will take that special girl to fix it all. Jill could be that one."

"Maybe ... but if I can't, uh, perform ... she's definitely not going to stick around. Why would anyone?"

Poor guy. He'd been really screwed up.

"Just go down on her. She'll love that. But don't do the alphabet trick. Never do that."

"Why would you ever do that? It doesn't work. Only the suck and blow method, I've found that to be successful." His face is so earnest when he says it that I have to crack up.

"Tell me you didn't research cunnilingus."

He grins proudly. "I've read four books on it, and I can say that I've never had a disappointed customer."

I drop my head in my hands, chuckling. "Of course you have."

Just two guys, talking about their lack of sex education in the middle of the neonatal intensive care unit.

35

ERIN

The day that Morgan and Jeff were finally able to bring Carina home from the hospital, Mom and I set up a little intimate brunch at our family home.

I'd done so much Pinterest research for this coming home party, and documented almost all of it on my Instagram stories on the blog. I'd told Morgan she was under strict orders not to watch them, or look at my blog posts, until they got here. Sure, I could have waited until after, but when you were handmaking wood letters covered in fake flowers that spelled out your niece's name, and you were a lifestyle blogger, you have to document that shit.

"Is this straight?" Reese stood on a chair, wobbling as he hung a canvas banner that read Welcome Home. I'd cut and sewn that myself ... this homecoming party had really brought out my inner-Martha Stewart.

"As an arrow." I smirked, and he turned his head to look at me.

Reese stepped off the chair and sauntered over to me, his hips conveying just what we were both thinking about. Thank God my mother was in the other room.

"Are you in the gutter over here, peas?" Those big hands gripped either side of my waist, squeezing gently.

The sensation was between a tickle and a pinch, and it sent a sizzle of lust to my core. It was no longer weird that we were sleeping together because ... well, the sex was just too good. Why had we waited this long to do this, again?

My heart fluttered a little thinking about lying in bed with him, like we'd been doing night after night. We'd been living at each other's apartments, a few days at one, and then a few days at the other. I wasn't sure, before we'd started this back when I was contemplating the pact, how it would work. Relationships had always intimidated me, given me a nauseous feeling, and not the good butterflies kind. But with Reese, it was just an extension of our friendship. We'd melted into dating and exclusivity like it was the next natural progression. I still don't think I believe that love conquers all or that soul mates will always be destined to find each other, but maybe my view on love is softening. Maybe it exists, if it's right.

Why had I spent so much time denying that with Reese, it would be right?

Not to say that I wasn't cautiously optimistic. Because I was extremely cautious. He still annoyed me daily, I wanted half an hour of alone time when I got home from work, and there definitely wasn't enough closet space for my shoes and his to coexist ... but we were working on it every day. And his little admission that he'd always had a crush on me, that he'd wanted to do this for a long time, it reassured something in me. That he didn't just fall on this idea because of this pact, or because he had been sick of Renée. Reese had always wanted me, but I'd been too intimidating to pursue it.

"And if I am?" I winked up at him.

"Maybe I need to lie down with you in that gutter. Quick,

they've got a spare bedroom somewhere around here, don't they?"

I grind my ass into the front of his plaid shorts, and he inhales a sharp breath. "Oh, yeah, that'd be appropriate. Welcome home, we're just banging it out for a second. Be right there!"

I pull away from him, and he tries to chase me, a giggle working its way up through my throat.

"Hello!" Morgan's voice sounds from the front door, and we hear footsteps.

I point my finger at Reese, threatening him silently not to start any funny business with me because they were home. He takes one step forward, biting his lip and making his dimple pop. He was the devil.

They walk into the kitchen, Morg looking like a beam of starlight she's so happy, with Jeff trailing behind her, carrying the baby in her car seat.

"Welcome home!" I cry, going to hug my sister. And then pushing her aside so I can see the baby. "Oh my gosh, look how cute you are in your little Janie and Jack outfit!"

I'd found this adorable blue and white dress that made her look like a little Parisian girl. I'd told Morgan that she better put it on her to bring her home or I'd boycott.

I wouldn't really have, but I haven't been able to do a photo shoot with my niece because she was in the NICU and I've been dying to. Today was my opportunity to post a hundred Instagram pictures of her.

"Can I hold her?" I smile at Jeff.

"Of course." He nods, starting to unstrap her.

My brother-in-law is a more reserved kind of man, although we've always gotten along. He's given me some great advice about how to redesign my website, or make it more user-friendly with blog posts, sale alerts and even linked my social media to it when I could not figure it out. And we bond over our mutual love of Morgan, so he's always been all right in my book.

As he puts her in my arms, she rubs her little eyes, opening them for two minutes and then nodding back off to sleep. She is so perfect, and I can't express how happy I am that she's finally home and out of the hospital. I can't even imagine how my sister feels. She's a fucking warrior. All moms are, and even though I'm not one, having a niece gives me a bigger appreciation for everything they do.

"So, we wanted to ask you two something ..." Morgan looks at Carina while I hold her, my niece covered in blue and eyelet from head to toe.

Her fashion sense has already made her auntie proud. Reese and I blink at them, waiting for the question.

Morgan and Jeff look at each other, and then at us. "We wanted to know if you would be Carina's godparents?"

My heart warms, but not for me. I knew I'd be her godmother, hell, I'd have been pissed if I wasn't. But the fact that they're asking Reese ... they're really including him as part of the family. Not that he isn't, he was a member of it far before Jeff. But it just solidifies that even if we aren't together, he is an integral part of Carina's life.

"Of course," I say at the same time Reese says, "Seriously?"

I look at him, his expression dumbfounded. "You guys want me to be her godfather?"

I swear, he's about to cry.

"You took such good care of her in the NICU, and you're already part of the family, Reese's Pieces. So yes, of course we want you to be her godfather."

Reese lays a hand on Carina's forehead. "I promise I'll always support and protect her."

Jeff walks over and shakes his hand, a look of manly oath passing between them.

"Great, you're making him more of a sentimental nerd than he already was. Thanks for that. What're you, Iron Man?" I rolled my eyes at them.

Reese's eyes light up. "I'm more of a Steve Rogers, not a Tony Stark. But I'm proud of you for your Avengers knowledge, peas."

I grumble, "That's because you made me watch them all back-to-back in the last month."

Morg laughs. "You guys are so cute."

I pretend to make a gagging noise, and then look at my niece. "Carina, never fall in love. It makes you weak. Except when it comes to you. I'll love you until the end of time. Until the Met Gala and skinny jeans cease to exist."

"Yeah, because those are the important things in life." Reese chuckled.

W hen we're young, we think birthdays are the be all end all.

And I guess, for me, this birthday is the be all end all.

Since the day we made the pact, I've thought about my thirtieth birthday every year I blew out candles on my birthday cake. For my eighteenth, when Erin and I were about to venture off to separate colleges. My twenty-first, in a tequila-induced haze, watching Erin sway on the dance floor. While I was away from her on my twenty-eighth, sitting across from Renée.

I thought about what this birthday would bring. Whether we would already be married, to each other or to other people. Would she be gone forever? Or sitting by my side?

And here she was, doing the latter. In a pink willowy dress, outside at the local brunch place in our hometown. We sat across from our respective mother, having promised to take them out for breakfast to celebrate our own birthdays.

But really, this was just a front. Because today was the day. My thirtieth birthday. The day I'd been thinking about and wishing for when I blew out candles for so many years. This little breakfast was all a front to get Erin right where I wanted her. In our hometown, in front of our moms.

This was where I wanted to propose. In one of the places that we'd spent so many moments in our childhood. Sunday brunches were a thing of the past at this tiny cafe off of Main Street, but if I had my way, I'd bring them back. I wanted her to be surprised, but not embarrassed. Erin wasn't the hot air balloon proposal type of girl. Really, she wasn't a proposal girl at all. Even though she loved a well-placed, girly Instagram photo.

I watch as she chats with our mothers, showing them her latest blog post on the flower arrangement class she'd done and documented. She'd smelled like fresh blooms for a week, and I'd loved it.

The crinkling package in my pocket felt like a weight, and I couldn't wait to slide it onto her finger.

I'd tricked her, not bringing anything up on her own birthday that we'd celebrated two weeks ago. We'd gone to Atlantic City, the Borgata if you're getting technical. I'd gone all out, getting us a room, booking reservations at this swanky Asian restaurant, sitting at the blackjack table for half the night and then going out dancing with her. I didn't make mention of the pact the entire weekend, and I wasn't sure if she noticed or she just didn't say anything because she didn't want to address it either.

We'd come home, and for two weeks, I'd acted normal. Coming home from work to her. Going out to the occasional dinner. Fucking like bunnies trying to win a race.

But in the back of my mind, I was planning. And plotting.

"Reese?" All three sets of eyes look at me expectantly.

"I'm sorry?" I can feel the sweat trickling down the back of my neck.

Erin squeezes my hand under the table. "Do you know what you're going to get for breakfast?"

I'm not even remotely hungry, the sudden burst of nervous energy hitting me like a tidal wave. My stomach rocks like I'm seasick on a Disney Cruise, and I grip Erin's hand a little too hard.

But something in me pulls me out, forcing me to recover. "What I always get, the western omelet."

My mom rolls her eyes. "That thing is massive ... I always wondered how you stayed so slim, my boy."

"Good genes." I wink at her.

Both moms melt and say, "*awwww*."

We put our orders in, and the conversation turns to the latest network television drama they're all watching. I tune them out, waiting for the exact moment I want to do this.

My opportunity opens after our server brings over the second round of mimosas. Well, mimosas for them, black coffee for me.

I feel like I'm about to pass out as I back up discreetly, each squeak of a chair leg on the linoleum sounding like a gunshot to my ears. I begin to pull the package from my pocket. It was now or never. Erin probably wasn't ready, but I'd been dragging her along with me in this pact and relationship for this long, so I'd have to push her into one more thing.

Kneeling beside my chair, I see Erin's eyes go wider than the state of Texas. "What are you doing?"

I keep going, sinking down onto my left knee as our mothers look toward me, confusion marring their expressions.

My eyes are trained on Erin. She's freaking out, but she hasn't bolted out of the room yet, so that's a good sign. Meanwhile, my heart is racing like I just did a marathon on crack ... not that I'd know how either of those things felt.

"Erin, from the first moment I saw you, I knew you would be my wife someday. And you thought I'd look good with a mud pie on my head, so perhaps we both predicted what would come true."

At this point, my mom is sobbing loudly in the background of my proposal, and I haven't even asked or taken a ring out yet.

"Oh my God ..." Her brown eyes are the definition of shocked, and I look her over, looking at the woman who has frequented so many days of my life.

"I can't think of any other person I'd want to spend the rest of my life with. You're my best friend, after all. I'll never find anyone who puts up with my lack of social media presence, or who'll give me the last bite of funfetti cake. And in return, I promise that I'll rub your feet after you're in heels for six hours, and that I'll wash the dishes because you only like to dry. So Erin Carter, will you please marry me? Make me the happiest man in the world?"

I pull out the ring in my pocket, or well ... the plastic in my pocket. Ripping open the Ring Pop packaging, I hold out a cherry Ring Pop, Erin's favorite flavor when we were growing up.

And to my surprise, she starts laughing. Cackling actually, big belly laughs as she holds out her hands to mine and grabs my wrists, anchoring herself.

"How did you know this was the exact ring I wanted?" She looks at me, my girl, my peas, sharing the jokes that only we understand.

"Do I know you? A skywriter proposal was never in the cards for us. So ... what is your answer?" I lean in and up, pressing my forehead to hers.

She touches my cheek, and I know that I've persuaded her. With the Ring Pop, putting a bit of our childhood fun into it, I've shown her how a marriage would be between us. This is what I wanted, how I planned to win her over.

"Yes. Yes, I'll marry you," Erin whispers, and our mothers cheer.

"Oh my God, I can't believe it! We have a wedding to plan! I'm getting a daughter, finally. Erin, do you like pink or purple flowers? Are we going to do the ceremony outside or in a church? DJ or band?"

My mom starts spouting off questions at a hysterically rapid pace, wondering aloud about every minute detail of the big day. That we haven't even discussed yet. Or even thought about. You know, since we just got engaged less than a second ago.

Barbara is pulled into a hug by my mom and I see it, that look of doubt in her eyes. I make sure to remind myself to keep Erin far away from her.

"I can't believe you got me a Ring Pop." Erin marvels at it as I slide it onto her ring finger.

"We can get you a real diamond later, but I figured you'd like this shiny baby for now." Bending in close, I whisper, "Plus, you can suck on it."

She squeezes my knee hard, and I realize I'm still kneeling. When I sit back in my chair, her eyes have heated and I know we'll be going at it as soon as we're alone. Since discovering sex with each other, it's like we've realized that this whole other side to our relationship exists. One that we'd deprived ourselves of and were now gorging on like the Halloween candy your parents hid for half the year and you accidentally found.

"Me and you getting hitched. Who would have thought?" Her eyes twinkle, and I hope that she's as happy as I am right now.

"I did!" Mom pipes up.

She captures Erin's attention, and I can't help but admire the way my new fiancée, damn is that weird to say, humors my mother.

I need to walk away for a minute, to fully bask in the moment, and I bring my coffee cup for a refill. Nothing like wedding talk and three women to make a man feel tired.

Barbara pulls me aside as I fill my mug, while my mom and Erin start talking about dresses and cakes. To her credit, she's trying to sound like a bride while looking super overwhelmed but happy to talk about all of the pink.

"Reese, I'm happy for you." Her cautious expression says otherwise.

"Thank you." I squeeze her hand where it rests on my arm, knowing that something more is coming

"But ... be careful with her heart. Love can be fickle. I hope you two outlast what most can't." She shrugs and has this fake sympathetic look on her face.

I'm instantly annoyed. Both by her warning, and I'm even more annoyed that's she annoyed me in this moment when I should be nothing but happy.

"Actually, I've always been careful with your daughter's heart. And I am realistic enough to know that marriage is a hard game, one that is played for the rest of one's life. But I've always been good to Erin, and she's always been good to me. Our friendship has outlasted many things and many years, and now we're going to deepen our connection. But it doesn't mean anything is changing. You need to be happy for your daughter."

Her eyes are a mixture of scolded puppy and jaded divorcée. "I hope you're right about all of that."

She's almost burst my bubble, but I buck up and refuse to let her. Taking my mug back to the table, I listen to Erin and Mom talk about Pinterest ideas and dress shops around the area.

I lace my fingers through Erin's under the table, and my heart swells as she leans into me, almost subconsciously. And I know we've done it. We've turned into those affectionate people who subtly touch each other without realizing it.

And now that she's wearing my Ring Pop, we'll get to touch each other, subtly or not, for the rest of our lives.

Y ou know how sometimes, you looked around at your life, and didn't really understand how you got to the place you were in at that exact moment?

That's how I felt right about now. Sitting in my sister's kitchen, her baby in a carrier around her shoulders, a pink silicone ring that Reese had found in a shop the other day was sitting on the fourth finger on my left hand. I'd almost preferred the Ring Pop.

Me, the romance naysayer, was about to plan a wedding. The one event in a woman's life that was all about flowers, kisses, sappy songs and love. That four letter word that I swore I'd never believe in.

I sat on one of the leather stools that surrounded her island, and watching as Morg prepared a salad while popping her boob out to stick in Carina's mouth.

"Talk about multitasking." I chuckled.

"The kid wants to be glued to my chest all day since she got home ... I can't say no. And even if I feel like a cow, breast milk is cheaper than formula." She shrugs, cutting a cucumber as my niece chomps on her nipple.

"Doesn't it hurt?" I grimace, holding my own boobs.

"Eh, you get used to it. Speaking of things we all have to get used to, I seriously can't believe you're actually engaged to Reese Collins. Reese's Pieces, the boy who once peed on our swing set out back because we wouldn't let him use our Barbie's as cannon fodder."

I burst out laughing. "I'd forgotten about that. Thanks for the image."

Not wanting to voice my internal thoughts, I turn back to my computer, pretending to work while she cooks. I spend a good chunk of time over here now, since Morgan's on maternity leave and I can work from anywhere.

But the thoughts I've been having are dangerous. And I'm afraid if I give them life by speaking them out loud, they'll grow legs and carry the whole thing away.

In my head, I go over it again. How I'm faking that I love to wedding plan. How it's been two weeks since Reese got down on one knee, and I haven't opened one magazine or gift that has been sent. How I loved the likes I got on Instagram for my engagement post more than I loved looking at rings with Reese. How every time we had sex now, I thought about our wedding night, and got a feeling of dread.

I'm not sure what switch flipped in my head after he popped the question, but as we were taking the train back to the city from our hometown, my stomach began to sink. I got this clawing feeling up the back of my throat, and then it felt like someone soaked my brain in anxiety acid. And every single day since, I'd had a moment where I felt like my lungs were closing in on themselves. Like I couldn't function. Like I'd never move again due to the panic seizing my body.

That feeling ... it brought on thoughts. Thoughts like, my life wasn't so bad. Why did I want to chain it to someone else's, even if it was someone like Reese who I loved and respected? Was I really going to get married? I didn't even believe in the institution ... so why was I going to go and commit to it?

"Have you spoken to Dad again?" Morgan asks, sipping a glass of wine now as she poured me one too.

It was two p.m., but I wasn't going to argue. Hell, I downed half of mine as soon as she put it in front of me. She wasn't pregnant anymore and she explained that she would pump and dump after so it was okay to have a glass every now and then while nursing and I was in the midst of an emotional panic, so we had earned this chardonnay.

Was it terrible that I would rather talk about my traitorous father than my impending marriage? That was how much I was freaking out about being engaged.

"We had two phone calls, and he wants to meet for coffee. He sent a congratulatory card ... I just still don't know where to put him." My feelings had warmed slightly, but we were still in Alaska when it came to cordiality. Maybe Alaska in spring, but still Alaska.

Morg nods. "That's okay, you don't have to know where to put him right now. The most important thing is that you're talking. That you're being open to it. Believe me, it wasn't easy for me when I was in your shoes. But I knew that I'd regret it, and you will too if you keep this cold shoulder up."

"Yeah, you're right ..." I'm distracted, thinking more about Reese than my dad.

She stops what she's doing and looks straight at me, with those big sister eyes that can practically see into my soul. "Are you sure you're okay with this whole engagement thing? I love you and Reese, and I love you together, but you don't have to get married just because of this pact."

How the fuck can she tell? She's eerily good at reading people for an accountant. Maybe she's secretly a spy or contract killer, like Ben Affleck in that one movie.

But I made a pact. I said I'd do it. And he asked. How could I say no to Reese? We were best friends, but would he ever forgive me if I broke this off? Something inside of me said no.

So I would go through with it. Because I loved him, even if we hadn't said those words. Even if I still wasn't sure if it was in the best friend way or the man of my dreams way.

"I'm getting married because I love him." I smile, trying to fake it as much as humanly possible.

It's the truth and the lie all wrapped into one. At this point, I can't tell which is which.

F inally a Friday that Reese had off from work, and I'd wanted to go out to this trendy lounge bar I'd been reading about.

The place had cocktails with chilis and bee pollen in them, liquor imported straight from Russia, and a band playing that was supposed to be the next up and coming thing in Philly. I wanted to go desperately, thought it would be a fun blog post for my followers.

But Reese had said he was tired, that we could just stay in and cook dinner together.

Nothing sounded more boring to me at this moment. It had instantly put me in a bad mood, and I was kind of sulking through the kitchen.

Reese cuts up the onions, and tells me that I need to start browning the meat. "Um, what?"

"Brown the meat." He doesn't look up.

I bite my lip to stop the chuckle, but it comes out anyway. "Is that supposed to be a euphemism for something? Because if you actually want me to cook, you should know that I don't. I mean, remember that time I burnt ramen in the microwave?"

It's his turn to chuckle. "Shit, you forgot to put water in it. Who does that?"

"Me. Still want to marry me?" I looked down at the simple silicone ring.

My head spun, I kind of couldn't believe that we were actually going to do this. The lies I'd been telling were catching up with me. But before I'd agree to marry him for real, I told him I needed a big fat diamond. Hell, I was a girl who ran a fashion blog ... did you really think I wouldn't be vain enough to want to pick out a fat ole engagement ring? And ... it was another stall tactic.

Reese looked at me, his hazel eyes heavy with thought. "Why, do I have more convincing I need to do?"

His tone might sound like it was trying to come off teasing, but I could hear the harshness underneath. "Chill, I was just kidding."

But I think I struck a nerve. Reese is chopping harder now, and something in the air has shifted. "No, really, Er. What else do I need to do? Because I've been pretty clear about my feelings, my intentions. And yet you still make jokes. And if we're being serious, you definitely still have doubts. I see it whenever I bring up any kind of planning question. You still haven't picked a date or a venue, you don't even want to talk about it."

It looks like somebody else in the kitchen has been hiding things too, and he can see right through mine. I'm completely blindsided, but I'd be lying if he hadn't identified a feeling I'd had deep down ever since I'd said yes to his proposal.

"Okay, bridezilla, calm down. I was seriously just kidding. I didn't realize it was such a big sticking point with you. We can talk about whatever you want."

But Reese wouldn't drop it. I could see the fire blazing in those hazel pools, the veins in his neck beating in time with his rapid heart rate. "I guess you just figure that if things don't work out, we could always just get a divorce!"

Everything in the room freezes. Time, my hands, my heart, Reese. The only thing making any noise is the stove burner I just flicked on to start the taco meat.

My mouth hangs open at the word ... the one word in the English vocabulary that can bring more pain to me than any other word. My stomach is ice, and yet I feel like I might bend at the middle and empty my guts all over his hardwood floors. Tears prick the corners of my eyes, and we're just staring at each other.

Reese starts to move, like a TV that has been unpaused. "Erin, no, I'm sorry, I didn't mean that ... work, today, it was terrible. I lost one of my babies, I'm so sorry, that is never an option, not to me ..."

He's stumbling over his words, walking around the island in his kitchen to get to me. But I just keep backing up, retreating.

"Baby, I'm sorry. I shouldn't have said that, it was an asshole thing to say. My temper got the best of me, I would never, I should have never said that word."

He reaches for me, and my voice is deadly quiet. "Do not touch me."

"Erin, come on, I'm sorry ..." He's begging like a puppy dog, but my heart has turned to stone.

"Fuck you. Fuck you for even thinking that *that* would be an option. You really think that?" I choke on a sob, grabbing my coat as I continue to back away from him.

"Of course not." Reese tries to reach for me again, and I swing my elbow away so he can't catch it.

"You wouldn't have said it if a tiny part of you didn't at least think it." My heart was crumbling, turning to ash.

I'd put myself out there, digested the thought of acting on the pact, dated him, opened my heart in a way that I never really wanted to. I had begun to come around to the idea of love, and by the time we got married, I honestly think I would have been settled with Reese the way he was with me. But now?

I couldn't wait to get as far away from him as possible.

He'd just said the word he could never take back, and for me, it was the breaking point.

I grabbed my bag, slid into my shoes and walked out the door.

Reese knew me well enough not to come after me.

W hen you're a nurse, you see the toll that drugs take on people.

In my clinical rounds as a nursing student, I'd seen a number of addicts who'd overdosed or were in the middle of a detox come into the hospital. They were out of their minds, on another planet, devoid of feeling pain or listening to rational thoughts.

Right now, I envied them. I wish I could take something that would shut this off, take away the agony pumping through me at all hours. I would do anything to rewind the past three days, to say something different, to make sure my feelings were so well heard that there would be no doubt on Erin's part that I'd been joking.

But deep down, I'd been waiting for this. The other shoe to drop. The straw to break the camel's back. The reason that Erin ends this ... I've been secretly anticipating it.

From the jump, the minute I mentioned the pact, I knew that we were heading for a momentous decision. It was either a happily ever after, or the end of an era.

And now, I had my answer. I sat on my couch, not even

watching the droning sports game that was on TV. I just had it on in the background, because it seemed like a normal thing to do right now.

Except ... right now wasn't a normal time. I had fucked-up. Fucked-up so bad that I'd lost my fiancée and my best friend all in the same sentence. I hadn't meant to say it. It had been a joke, albeit an insensitive one.

But I'd seen her eyes. How she'd shut down. She had never, in our lives, looked at me like that. I'd watched her do it to other people, but I'd never been on the other side of that mistrusting stare.

My heart was ripped to shreds. And I had eaten an entire Turkey Hill container of Party Cake. So my stomach was being ripped to shreds as we spoke.

A knock on my door has my head whipping up, my heart galloping at the thought of seeing Erin on the other side. Maybe she'd come to tell me she was sorry she'd overreacted. More likely, she'd come to punch me in the balls for using the word divorce when it applied to us. I'd take either happily.

Except when I swing it open, my face screws up like I've just eaten a lemon.

"What're you doing here, Renée?" I don't say it to be rude, I guess I'm just completely shocked.

If you looked up the definition of "just-had-sex hair," there would be a picture of Renée. Dark black curls that spread down her back like inky silk, with eyes almost the same color, she looked like a sun-kissed Victoria's Secret Model. She was gorgeous, probably one of the best looking women I'd ever dated.

But she was also high-maintenance and vapid in a way that could be downright nasty at times.

"Hi, sweetheart, good to see you too. Remember our text conversation? I said I wanted to get together. Well ... I never heard from you so I figured I'd make the trip out to see you face-to-face."

Did I also mention she could be batshit crazy when she wanted to be?

"Um ... you should have told me you were coming." I was still kind of dumbfounded.

She waltzed in, looking around. "Now why would I do that? We would have argued, and you hate it when we argue."

"We don't argue anymore. We're not together." I often had to remind her of reality.

"Nice place, by the way. A little masculine for my taste, but it's nice. How have you been, baby? I've missed you."

For the first time since we broke up, I realize that I haven't missed her. Not one bit. But she's missed me, and it's nice to be missed. It's better than being doubted and teased every moment like I was with Erin.

Could I do this with her? Wouldn't it be easy? A thousand times easier than trying to cajole and convince Erin? Renée and I had been good together. A little tepid, a little fake at times, but we had laughs and good sex and she took care of me.

"Do you want anything? A glass of water, a beer?" I figure if she's flown all the way here, the least I can be is courteous.

She chuckles. "I always did love the way you said water. More like *wooder,* with that Philly accent."

I walk to the fridge with no response, because she was always annoying about my "accent." There she was, dropping bless your hearts and y'alls like it was a religion, but the way I said water was funny. It makes me snap back to myself, and I don't want any part of this. I want Erin.

"I'm with someone, Renée." Because in my mind, Erin and I had just hit a speed bump, not a dead end.

"Seriously?" She scoffs, looking pissed. "Already? Jeez, Reese,

I knew you were a player, but to be in another relationship so fast?"

My smile is tight and grim. "Renée, I haven't even seen you in five months. One, that's not that quick. Two, I'm not a player. Three, I'm surprised you didn't see it since you stalk her blog religiously."

I can't help but drop Erin's blog into the conversation. Renée always got so jealous when I brought up how well my best friend was doing in her entrepreneurial endeavors.

"Wait ... you're seeing Erin?" Her eyes go livid with that big green monster stomping around in her brain. "Well, maybe she can finally tame the ladies' man. Hell knows I couldn't, and I'm way more beautiful than her."

Her voice is grating on my nerves, and I want her out. Now. "Do not ever talk about her that way in my presence ever again. In fact, I'm busy. It was good to see you."

It really wasn't, and I started walking her to door.

"Maybe she's good for you. She's watched you flirt with other women for years, so maybe it's okay in her book."

In that moment I hated her, because she was holding up a hypothetical mirror to my face. For so many years, I'd gone from girlfriend to girlfriend, discarding them when I got bored. Subconsciously, Erin had probably watched it all through her lens of disillusionment. Did she think that I was going to do that to her?

I managed to push Renée out, all but slamming the door in her face. Just as quick as she'd spun in, did she spin out. And in the process, had restored a fight in my pathetic, sulking heart.

I had to get to Erin. I had to tell her that she was my only one. That she'd only ever been my only one.

Where she has doubts, I have none. Where she has given up, I'll fight. For us.

40

Typically, the one person I would call at a time like this was Reese.

That's what I got for deciding to fall in love with my best friend.

Reese and I hadn't spoken in three days, not since I dashed out of his apartment. So far, I'd been through three bottles of wine, two pints of coffee ice cream, and four seasons of *The West Wing*. I had vowed never to be that mopey, depressed, heartbroken girl when it came to getting over a guy.

But I hadn't accounted for being heartbroken over the one guy in my life that meant everything to me, not just as a fiancé either. Any other fuckboy, I could have just gotten over. Probably would have gone complaining to Reese about how all men were the same, and why couldn't I just sleep around and not conform to society's pressure to marry.

Except ... that fuckboy was Reese. And he really wasn't one, he was just an insensitive asshole. He is my fiancé, or at least he was. I hadn't even wanted to be engaged or in a relationship with him mere months ago, and now I couldn't fathom what I was going to do without him. Without our relationship.

Because the truth was, I didn't just miss my best friend. I missed my boyfriend. The man I was going to marry. The one who had spooned me in bed for the last couple of months even though he knew I didn't really like it and got overheated. I used to slide out of his grasp as soon as he fell asleep, kissing his nose before turning over and spreading out like a starfish.

I missed holding hands while we walked to our bench in the park with donuts. I missed his cooking, since I'd eaten nothing but junk food on my couch this week. I missed how he knew every single thing about me, and me about him.

I didn't just miss having my childhood friend. I missed everything that was going to come for us.

How pathetic was I? I'd become the very thing I'd always tried to avoid.

And although Reese had been insensitive to my history with divorce, if I hadn't reacted the way I did, we wouldn't be in this position. We would have talked it out, annoying each other like we always had. He'd call me a brat and I'd call him a dick. And then we would have apologized and had sweaty makeup sex or something.

I'd have to tell Morgan soon. I'd been hiding out in my apartment like it was a bomb shelter or something. I'd have to take the ring off. I'd have to tell my followers, something that made my cheeks heat in embarrassment. I'd already gone public with a perfectly staged engagement photo of my hand and Reese's. My followers were freaking out, and the amount of new followers I gained from that post was enough to put me on the radar of two fashion companies that were interested in using me as one of their brand reps. One of them was huge, and I was crossing my fingers it came through.

"Of course I'm still here, you asshole," I yelled at the TV when my Netflix went off, asking me that silly question.

And that's when I realized that I'd been inside for way too

long, and I needed to get out. My inner couch potato protested, and I pouted while tying my shoelaces on my sneakers, but once I got outside and began walking, I felt marginally better.

My headphones were plugged into my ears, an audiobook on Coco Chanel playing, when someone tapped my shoulder. I might have grown up outside the city, but I was a Philly girl through and through. I would cut a bitch if anyone got too close, especially in a park as the sun was setting.

I rip out an earphone and whirl around, while someone practically yells in my face.

"Oh my God, are you Erin Carter?"

"Uh, yeah ..." I'm still disoriented and confused.

The woman, a tall redhead that looks to be around my age, gushes, "I just love your blog! Gah, I must look like a total loser right now, but those Steve Madden sandals you posted last month? I bought them because of you! And they're amazing! Oh! Congratulations on your engagement, I absolutely love the story. Can I see your ring?"

I blush, both internally and externally, that I've been recognized. Is this what it's like to be famous? Because I could get used to this. And the fact that she just said she bought a pair of shoes because of me? That has me beaming with pride.

I hold out my left hand, Reese's face popping into my head and the moment he got down on one knee rippling over my memory. "It's just a placeholder right now."

What a lie. I was going to have to take off this rubbery piece of plastic soon.

"I love the story about how he asked with a Ring Pop." She winks at me.

"Thank you so much." I feel like a complete liar accepting her congratulations, knowing that Reese and I aren't speaking right now.

"Can I tell you something?" She looks nervous, like I might think it's weird if she confides something in me.

"Of course ..." I hope she doesn't tell me something too personal. I am bad at hiding that expression that looks like I'm uncomfortable and don't want to hear your business.

"I obviously don't know you well, but I've always admired your sarcastic tone while also giving great fashion finds. Like, you just seem like a totally normal girl to me. Not one of these prettily perfect bloggers who craps rainbows and has never had a broken nail. I honestly always thought, from your posts, that you didn't really like to have boyfriends. I'm not sure why, I just got that feeling. And then you post about Reese ... it just is so sweet! Makes you even more relatable. I guess I'm just trying to say that ... thank you for your blog. Somedays, it's the only thing that makes me smile."

I'm speechless. Which seriously, doesn't happen a lot for me. But I'm dumbstruck, not sure how to thank this woman for putting everything back into perspective for me. I thank her and keep walking, my chin tucked to my chest as my pace quickens.

What she said rang so true. I'm not perfect. I don't pretend to be. So why should my relationship be? Why should marriage be? Life was messy.

And as corny and rom-com as it sounded, I wanted my life to be messy with Reese.

I'm about to knock on Erin's door, when it suddenly opens.

I'm knocked back into the wall outside her door, my chest cushioning her running figure, an *ooph* coming from my throat.

Dark brown eyes blink up at me, her hands resting on my pecs. "I was just coming to see you."

"You were?" I hold her against me, breathing in her scent and feeling her warmth.

I missed her so much, and it's only been three days. I don't think we've ever gone three days without talking in our lives, except when she'd accidentally jumped in a pool with her phone in her pocket during an impulsive, drunken night in college.

"I had to talk to you." Her hands scale up my back, like they need my shirt to disappear so they can feel my skin.

"Can I come in?" I look down at her from where I tower a head above her.

She nods, and it's one of the only times that I feel like Erin is shy.

Before we even fully make it inside, I'm the picture of contrition. "I'm so sorry, peas. I should have never said what I said. I didn't mean it, you know that. I know that you know that. When I said I wanted to marry you, I meant that I wanted to be with you forever. I know we joke and make fun of love, but I do. I love you."

Erin throws her hands up, walking away from me. "Why do you even want to do this? You could have any little preppy housewife, who would fold your clothes and cook your meals. If it has something to do with honoring the pact, you're off the hook. Seriously, Reese."

"Yeah, I could have any other woman, and she'd be a hell of a lot less difficult than you."

Erin huffs, annoyed. "Yeah, you could. So go get one."

"But I don't want anyone else. I want you. I always have. You want the truth? I'll give it to you."

Wrapping her arms around her body in a self-defense move, she looks unsure, like she needed to brace herself for this.

"I had a crush on you the first time I ever saw you. I just agreed to be best friends because you asked, giving me a mud pie to celebrate, and I wanted to be as close to you as I could possibly get. And over the years, whenever I tried to tell you, I chickened out. You're strong as hell, and have always known what you want and how to get it in the most determined fashion. What if I messed things up? I couldn't think about a life without you in it, so I just kept quiet ... kept things the way they were. But every time you went out with someone else, each time you said that love was a farce and you didn't believe in it, it killed me a little inside."

I may sound dramatic about all of this, but I have to get my point across. To show Erin that I've always been here, waiting quietly. I have to suck in a breath, because this next part is the scariest thing I've ever done.

"The night I fell in love with you? That party at Mitch Callister's house, remember the party down by the river? We were freshman and it was the first senior party we'd gotten invited to, and we had foamy keg beer. Mitch noticed you, knew you were Morgan's sister. He flirted with you, and you were gawking at him. I knew then, with that big green monster on my back, that I had to do something. That I had to have some kind of insurance policy, because I was in love with you. And do you remember what I did the next morning? We were sitting in your backyard, and I proposed the pact. Because I wanted to make sure, that after it all, after we grew and made mistakes and sowed our oats, that we would come together. Because I'm in love with you. I've been in love with you for a very long time. And it doesn't have to be that romantic, sweep you off your feet, take a bullet for you love ... although I'd do that. Love can be quiet and patient. It can wait for the other person to be ready, while also laughing and spending time with that person. That's why I want to fulfill the pact, because I actually meant it when I proposed it at fifteen. You're the only one I've ever wanted to marry. It's probably why I could never get a relationship right, because I was just biding my time until you softened to the idea."

Slowly, I walk to her, kneeling down again in front of her on one knee. When I take her left hand, I notice she hasn't taken off the pink silicone ring I'd picked out as a placeholder.

"I've only ever loved you, Erin. I realize you may have seen me with other women, but you are it for me. I'm yours. Whether you want me or not now, I will never be with anyone else. You are my end game, the reason I put that pact in place. I would have never married anyone else. And on the lucky chance that you hadn't, I had my insurance. Times up, we're here. I love you. I'm in love with you. I didn't say that the first time I proposed, but I love you. I should have started with that. I am in love with you. Marry me. Be my partner, my best friend."

Looking up at her, I see the tear that streams down her

cheek. She touches it, looking at the tear on her finger and then me. "You made me cry."

I've only ever seen her cry three other times in all the years I've known her. "Does that mean I broke you?"

"I think it means you fixed me." Erin huffed, looking up at the ceiling. "God, that sounded cliché. But ... I guess I am. Because I'm going to marry the boy next door like some kind of Meg Ryan movie. And by the way, I love you, too."

My mouth went dry and my hand tightened around hers. My other went to her ankle, sliding up her leg to the top of her tight black workout shorts. She'd answered my question with the exact three words I'd been waiting to hear since the day I'd met her.

There was nothing else to talk about. So I kissed her.

*H*ands on skin.

   Lips on flesh.

   Teeth biting into the inside of thighs.

Nails scraping down muscles.

It was all a blur as Reese and I went at it like wild animals, the kind of makeup sex that you only read about in books. The kind that breaks lamps and shakes the foundation of the earth and all of that other life altering crap.

One minute, we're standing in the entrance to my apartment that opens up into my living room. And the next, Reese is throwing me down on the bed after he picked me up, attacking my mouth at the same time as he walked. How could he see? How did he not walk us into a wall, or trip over the seven pairs of shoes littering my kitchen floor. You know that high that people get when they're on a crazy dangerous drug, the one that allows them to like, flip a car over? Maybe sex does that to Reese. Because if I had just attempted to foreplay with a woman while walking backward in an apartment that wasn't my own, I would have ended up with a concussion and a broken toe.

"Stop thinking," Reese growls, his eyes the most intoxicating shade of jeweled green, as he rips off the shorts I was wearing and dives in without another word.

And that right there makes me stop thinking. All I can focus on are his lips and tongue working me like a well-trained violin player plucking at the strings. Higher and higher, I'm making notes that I hadn't even known were humanly possible. Gasping for air as I writhe on my bed, trying to grind his face into me in such an unladylike way, it should be illegal. But I can't help it, my body just keeps making those motions.

"That's it, use my tongue." Reese smirks into my core, taunting me as I get so close, I ball my fists into his hair and pull hard.

I'm about to come undone, the tingles in my feet have started, when he comes up for air.

"No, no, no ..." I pant, annoyed.

Reese is naked in seconds flat, and then tugging at my shirt as he comes down over my body. "I want to see you come around my cock."

Oh. Well. Don't mind if I do, then. His words send a surge through me that threatens to have me coming before he even enters my body.

"Get inside me already," I whine, like a needy thing.

"Missed me, huh?" He smooths down my hair, slowing down when what I need for him is to be banged like a porn star.

"Yes, now fuck me."

"Not until you say it again."

"Say what? Fuck me?" I'm getting desperate.

"That you love me. Tell me that you love me." He's using his cockpower over me.

"That's not fair. You're withholding orgasms in exchange for something. First rule of marriage, never withhold orgasms."

He chuckles, fisting himself and running his cock up and down my slit, teasing me. "I'm going to give you your orgasm.

But not in exchange for anything, because technically, you've already given them to me. Come on, baby, say it."

"I love you." I have no fight in me to argue, I'm too wound up and need release.

Reese smiles, and then slams into me with such force that I'm unraveling before he even withdraws to stroke again.

He never lets up, not once. Bangs me just like a porn star, just like I needed. Exactly how makeup sex is supposed to be. And he even gives me another orgasm before he is biting my neck, jutting like he can't control his own hips.

"I love you," he says as he lets his own climax take over.

"Hi, Shoe Addicts! We're back for round two of Reese's Try Ons!" I spoke excitedly into my camera, happy that my cat eye came out so good today as I spoke.

I hit the screen and the camera flips around to Reese, who does a little booty shake in his tuxedo, the arms and legs a little too baggy and long for him right now.

"Hi ladies ..." Reese winks, and I can just imagine hundreds of women watching this on social media swooning. I know I did.

"We're trying on wedding tuxes today, and boy oh boy am I in heaven!" I pan the camera around the tailor's shop we found in the middle of downtown Philadelphia.

Reese had insisted on buying his tuxedo for the wedding, had said he wanted to own the suit he wore for our special day. As a non-romantic, I had rolled my eyes. As a fashion lover, I couldn't agree more.

After our come-to-Jesus moment where I realized I'd been stupid and irrational and that I was in love with Reese, and he'd realized he had been an asshole and had spilled his entire heart out to me, we had moved fast. Finding out that Reese had proposed the pact because he was always in love with me kind of opened up my eyes. It made me realize that what he'd said before was true, that some love was patient and complicated, not a story of roses and champagne. That was real, *we* were real.

And after that, he had insisted we get married as soon as possible. Unlike a lot of the other bloggers I knew in this line of fashion or lifestyle, I hadn't really ever thought about my wedding. I definitely hadn't planned it down to every last detail. I didn't know what kind of dress fit I'd like, didn't envision the perfect flower arrangement, and hadn't really had a preference when it came to church or no church.

Honestly, Morgan and Mrs. Collins had really been the driving force behind throwing together an impromptu wedding in two and a half months. They'd called a local venue in Wildwood, right off the beach, who just happened to have a cancellation. It was a beautiful mansion-looking building that was styled with a glass roof so that at night, we'd be dancing under the stars. We'd get married right on the beach we'd spent summers on.

Mrs. Collins had done all of the flowers arrangements, I'd only given her the colors. Blush pink and cream, simple and pretty. Turns out that one of Reese's other friends from high school, even though I don't remember him having other friends, owned his own photography and videography business, so we were set there.

Our favors would be Philly soft pretzels hung on a wall. Kind of like those donut walls that were all over Pinterest, but soft pretzels. The band was a splurge, but once I'd heard them in a YouTube video I'd found, I had to have them. Turns out they too had a cancellation for our weekend ... Reese said it was fated. I just thought we had dumb luck, but I didn't bicker about his rose-colored glasses.

I'd gotten my dress, an A-line long sleeved beauty that was covered in lace. My shoes, Manolo's, had been way too expensive. But these were the most important shoes of my life, I had to have them. We'd decided that I'd do my own hair and makeup, and that Morgan would be matron of honor, Preston would be Reese's best man, and Jeff would perform the ceremony. Carina would walk down in her mom's arms as our flower girl.

"What do you think about the all black, no pinstripe?" Johnny, the tailor of the shop we'd found, asks me.

Now all that's left to do is buy Reese's tux, and we're all set to get hitched two Saturdays from now.

"I think it's classic." I start an Instagram Live video. "What do you guys think? Just the sharp, classic black?"

Answers from my followers start rolling in, telling me that straight up black is the only way to go. Some say no, go navy or gray, it will complement better with his dark hair.

But when I look over, my eyes catching his green pools in the mirror, I think he looks edible in the traditional tuxedo. "What do you think, carrots?"

He smirks, his dimple popping. "I think I look like James Bond. Which reminds me, where are we going on our honeymoon? England, maybe? France? Or would you rather lie on a beach? I could look at you in a bikini all day."

I keep the video rolling while he gets fitted, pins and chalk marking the suit. "Hm, good question. Where should we go? I have never been to Europe, but I also know that I love to just lounge on the beach and begin drinking tequila at ten a.m."

"Or maybe picklebacks," Reese quips, our inside joke gaining a laugh from me.

My followers comment rapidly.

Antigua.

Paris.

Capri.

Aruba.

Bali.

I flip the camera around to selfie mode. "All of these places you guys are suggesting sound amazing, we'll have to decide where we want to go."

"It won't matter, peas. We'll be in the bedroom the whole time," Reese teases, but I see the heat in his eyes.

Laughter bubbles up from my throat, and my jaw drops. "I can't believe you just said that."

The tailor smiles at us like two kids in love, and my followers are going haywire on the live chat after his sexy confession.

We're at the store for another two hours, and we pay an arm and a leg to have the suit finished by Thursday, but it's worth it.

The only thing left to do is show up on our wedding day. Before we brought up the pact, before he'd sent me that email and come to town and kissed me, I would have doubted that I'd be walking down that aisle. In fact, I would have told you I'd be running the other way.

But not anymore. I was a cynic in love. A cynic who was going to marry her best friend.

The beach in mid-September was typically a chilly, on-the-cusp-of-winter sandbar. But thanks to global warming, we'd gotten a mild, sixty-five degree day for our wedding day.

It was a miracle that it had all come together, and by no part was I taking any credit for that. Sure, I'd posted pretty wedding planning pictures and gone above and beyond to document it all on my blog, but Morgan had done most of the leg work. Remind me to buy her a really nice pair of shoes after this.

We stood on the beach, the wind whipping around us, as the crowd of fifty or so wedding guests looked on. Jeff had already gone through the pleasantries, thanking everyone for coming, going over why we were here. We were here because two weirdos fell in love, and planned to live happily ever bickering.

I stood across from Reese, who looked dashing in his black tux, his green eyes wet after he saw me in my dress, walking down the aisle. I hadn't cried, I rarely did, but I did have that ball of emotion in my throat that threatened to bring on tears.

"I vow never to turn a *Star Wars* marathon off, even if a red carpet event is on. I vow to always dry the dishes, and to pick up the donuts before people watching. I will never laugh when you can't spell correctly, and I promise to always laugh at your made up song lyrics. I vow to be your best friend, your partner in crime, and your confidant. I will love you until my last dying breath, or something equally as dramatic. Hopefully it's not something out of a Dwayne Johnson film though, because you know how I feel about that. Last of all, I promise to put you before all else, even my favorite pair of shoes. You know me better than I know myself, Reese, and my heart has always been yours. Now it will be yours forever. Take care of me and know that I will take care of you."

My sappy man has unshed tears in his eyes when I gaze into them, hoping that he liked my vows. I get a dimpled smile and I know I've done well. I meant all I'd said, from the bottom of my unfrozen heart.

"Reese, would you like to make your vows to Erin?" Jeff said, and baby Carina cooed from my sister's arms.

Reese took a deep breath, squeezing my hands where we held on to each other between our bodies. Another wave crashed on the shore, and again, I thought that this couldn't be more perfect. Who was I? A teary bride on her wedding day, that's who. I was allowed to be all the kinds of cheesy and sentimental that I wanted to be today.

"From the first day that I saw you, I knew you would be the woman I married."

He stopped, because almost everyone in the crowd let out a collective *awwww*.

"And while it took you a little while longer to come to that conclusion, I was always waiting for you. Always protecting you. Always thinking about your needs, how to make you laugh, and to hold you when you were upset. Which was fairly hard since you often tried to slap me when I wanted to comfort you."

I couldn't help but laugh.

"You're an amazing ball of fire, light and energy, and I am so lucky just to stand right beside you. I promise that I will continue to be patient, continue to love you even when you refuse to throw out one of your two hundred pairs of shoes, and always let you eat the last handful of popcorn at the movies. I love you, Erin. Always have, always will. I can't wait to see what our future holds."

He squeezes my hands after he's done, and I barely register Jeff walking us through the traditional wedding vows and promises that we have to complete in order to make our marriage legal.

Only when it's almost over do I tune back in, so lost in Reese's expression that I'm not paying attention.

"I now present, Mr. and Mrs. Reese Collins. You may kiss the bride." Jeff stepped out of the way like we'd rehearsed. I didn't want him in my first kiss as a married couple picture. No offense to him.

The crowd whooped and cheered, but all I could think about were Reese's lips on my own. How much had we been through? How much was to come?

All I knew was, I got to wake up to my best friend every day. And prior to what I'd originally thought, that was a hell of a lot better than waking up alone. Of course it was, now there would be a hot, naked man in my bed from here on out.

As everyone filtered back up the beach, we posed for pictures, by ourselves and with my family. After, we made it to the last half hour of our cocktail hour, and then came dinner time.

The sun was setting by the time we entered the hall, doing our first dance to "The Way You Look Tonight" by Frank Sinatra. It was cliché and classic, but it was better than the *Star Wars* theme that Reese had wanted. I'd vetoed that one in a second.

My dad had come, although I'd walked down the aisle by

myself. I was an independent woman, making an independent choice to marry the man that I loved. My father and I weren't in the best of places, but we were lightyears from where we had been. I'd even agreed to a dance, but I got to pick the song. "You'll Be in My Heart" by Phil Collins, because Dad had always liked the movie *Tarzan* when Morgan and I were little girls. Reese had danced with his mom to "My Wish" by Rascall Flatts, and they'd both cried. Her more than him, she was practically a sobbing wet mess by the end of the song.

It was a bit tense between him and Mom, mostly because my mother had pitched a fit about it beforehand and Dad definitely knew her feelings toward him now. But, Morgan and Reese had intervened, having had a strongly worded talk with her, and she was behaving herself thus far.

"You better get over there and eat your dinner, peas." Reese sidles up to me on the dance floor, where I'm dancing with his dad and a couple of friends from college.

"I will, I will! You know I wouldn't miss out on my steak." I lace my hands through his where they wrap around the front of my waist.

He feels solid and warm, and with the champagne flowing through my veins, he's an anchor. I allow him to lead me to our sweetheart table, cut up a piece of steak, and feed it to me.

"You know this is a one-time occurrence, right? Usually, I'd be spearing that fork through your hand if you tried to touch my plate or food."

"Of course I know that, I remember the time you almost impaled me with a chopstick for putting a bit of wasabi on one of your designated sushi rolls."

Reese looks at me lovingly, and turns to his plate. We eat in contented silence as we watch our guests mill about or dance.

Jill and Preston glide around the dance floor together, and she's giggling at something he's said. I wonder if they ever overcame the hump that was Preston's lack of hump. Reese had filled me in on it, and I was rooting for the hot doctor to finally get it up. From the way they were looking at each other, I would say that it was a likely probability that he'd worked out his problems.

The evening extended, moving to the bar for an after party after the last dance song, The Mummer's "Strut," had been played.

The pretzel wall, our favors to our guests, was a huge success. Dozens of flavors, from cinnamon to jalapeño, from our favorite bakery in Philadelphia, all hung from hooks on an elaborate wooden board that stood seven feet tall and seven feet wide.

And then Reese and I ended our night in our hotel suite, on the balcony overlooking the beach. While most couples would have dived right into bed, my husband, oh my God, *husband*, wanted to christen that balcony.

Just my type of marriage, nowhere near boring or regular.

From one beach to another, our marriage blossomed under the sun.

I watched as Erin walked to our chairs in the shade of a tiki hut, her body glistening with fresh sea water, her long hair slicked down her back. My cock got hard, not that it wasn't hard for most of this damn vacation, and I had to readjust my bathing suit.

"You're giving me a boner, *again*." I reach for her as she sits down, biting her sun kissed shoulders.

"We just had sex," she guffaws, but leans over and finds my lips.

Her kiss is salty and wet, and I want to throw her over my shoulder and bring her back to our hotel room. I'd done it last night after dinner, and she'd screamed all the way there. A couple of other couples staying on the resort had smiled or winked at us, and I'd given a thumbs-up back at them.

We couldn't take a full honeymoon now because of my shifts and being under a year tenured at CHOP, but I did have four days off the week after our wedding. With Erin being able to work from anywhere, we decided to take a short trip to Bermuda, with a longer honeymoon sometime next year.

The pink sand and clear waters were perfectly fine for me right now. Well, and the hot as hell woman next to me.

"Do you want another dirty banana?" I ask her.

Erin smirks. "Is that supposed to mean something else?"

"I meant your drink, get out of the gutter." I flagged down a waiter and ordered her another frozen banana blended with Kahlua.

"Thanks, husband." She winks. "Isn't it weird that you're my husband?"

I hold her hand, watching the waves crash. "But in a way, it isn't."

"You're right." Those brown eyes look at me, understanding me more than anyone ever has.

"What was that? I'm right? I rarely hear those words." My smile is teasing.

"Oh, stop it. I'm a brand new Erin, I can admit when you have the better idea."

"It's only taken thirty years."

One of our phones begins to vibrate from deep within the beach bag, and she reaches in to fish it out. Holding it up, she examines her phone, because who would be calling me. I gave Preston strict instructions not to have anyone call me on this trip, no matter how much I loved my patients and coworkers.

"Hello, this is Erin," she answers her phone, always a professional.

For her, it's not just some random cruise line calling to tell you that you won a four-day vacation if only you'll buy this set of expensive knives. No, my wife got phone calls from brands and stores alike, so she had to answer random phone numbers unlike the rest of us. And yes, I was using the word wife every chance I got. I hadn't been allowed to do it for so long, and now I was. I was a kid in an unlimited candy store.

"Yes, thank you. I do love your pieces, that one fringe skirt got a lot of hits on my blog." Nodding her head, as if she's actually talking to them in person.

I begin to scratch my nails down her back, and I see her shoulders relax. She turns around and makes a satisfied face at me. Not able to resist her warm, tan skin, I begin to kiss and nibble at her shoulder blades. Erin waves me off, getting up to stand as she listens to whoever is talking on the other end of the phone.

"Wow, I don't mean to sound like an amateur, but I'm shocked. I would be very interested, thank you for this opportunity. What would it entail?"

As I watch her pace the sand in front of our chairs, my ears perk up. It's a business call, clearly. Something to do with the blog. And the way her jaw is simultaneously dropping and then breaking out into a smile, I can only assume it's good.

"Yes, please send me the contract and I can look it over once I'm back from my honeymoon." A pause. "Oh thank you, I got married a week ago. Yes, we're having a great time, thank you. Okay ... okay. Thank you again, I look forward to working with you."

Erin hangs up, and then pumps her fists in the air, jumping around. "Holy freaking shit!"

Getting up, my bones lazy from the sun, I join her on the sand. "What was that about?"

She runs her hands through her wet, cornflower hair. "Oh my God, LOFT wants to partner with me. LOFT, babe! My favorite clothing brand, a *huge* company. That means Ann Taylor, their parent company, is behind it. Oh my God, I feel like a total fangirl but this is so awesome."

Wrapping her in a hug, my own pride swells for her. She is

living her dream, a thing that not many people get to do. "I am so proud of you, this is amazing, peas."

She rambles on, still caught up in the phone call. "They want to contract me for two years. Ten percent of every item I sell through the links I provide my followers on my posts. That is a lot of money, babe. Clothes that they send me for every season. I am shaking ..."

"Let's get some champagne to celebrate. Maybe a bubble bath. Candles ..." My mind starts to wander to our bedroom again.

"Stop thinking about your cock at a time like this." Erin laughs and jumps into me, and I pick her up, carrying her to the water.

"I'm always thinking about it when it comes to you." I dunk us both.

We spend the next three hours floating in the ocean, talking about her blog, and drinking champagne tinged with salt water.

"Isn't seeing your husband's wedding ring a turn on?" Morgan muses to me, looking at my wedding band and engagement ring together.

"Yeah, I guess. But looking at my diamond is more of a turn on." I admire the round cut halo setting, watching the rainbows bounce off of it.

"You're such a materialist." She rolls her eyes.

I look up from my computer, raising an eyebrow. "I never claimed I wasn't. I like things. I like pretty things. So does everyone else, they just don't admit it. I'm vain enough to put my materialistic life out there, that's not a bad thing. Almost every single one of your mommy friends does the same … they love posting about makeup and shoes and purses. I just make money from it."

Morg stares at me. "You're evil, I swear. Maybe I shouldn't let my kid learn things from her godmother."

I stalk over to where Carina sits in her swing and pick her up, nuzzling her soft cheek with my nose. "Don't listen to your mommy. She's just jealous because I got better eyebrows than she did."

"Bitch ..." Morgan mumbled, and I laughed.

I cradled my niece, staring at her as she peeked up at me through those infant eyes that seemed sleepy and alert at the same time.

"What is it about getting married and finding your soul mate that makes you want to pop out babies that look like him and you?" I pondered, because ever since we'd gotten married, all I could think about was children that would like Reese and me.

Morgan picked a booger out of Carina's nose and wiped it on a tissue. "Oh, just wait until you actually have a kid. Then you'll want ten more just like it. And that's after my horrendous labor and Carina in the NICU. I can't imagine what a normal delivery is like, when you get to sweetly bond with your baby. And yet, I want to do it all over again. Still can't feel my stomach from the numbness of my C-section scar, but I'd do it again tomorrow to get a little boy who was just as cute as this girl."

She picked up my niece from my arms, admonishing me for waking her up, and planted a kiss on her nose before putting her in her swing, where Carina smiled and began to drool before nodding off to sleep.

"Women, and our bodies, are weird. Completely fucking cool and warrior-like, but so weird," I marveled.

"I still think about how she literally grew inside my body. It's so fucking weird, but so cool." Morgan shrugged and walked across the room, sitting down on the couch.

I followed to join her, taking out my phone and texting Reese before sitting down.

Erin: *Hey, what time will you be home tonight?*

"So, do you think you and Reese will move into a different apartment?" Morgan picked up a set of knitting needles.

I was so distracted by the homely activity, that I couldn't even concentrate. "Um ... probably eventually. His apartment is closer to the hospital so that's where we stay now, and I'll give up my apartment at the end of my lease. Then we'll probably look for a two bedroom close to the hospital. Or maybe something a little further from Center City. I'm sorry ... are you knitting?"

Morgan holds up what looks like a raggedy blanket. "Trying to, albeit badly. I'm so bored on maternity leave! And I thought this would be a fun mommy kind of thing to do, so I tried to pick up knitting. Except I suck at it, and this looks more like a holey sock than a baby blanket."

"Okay, stop that immediately. We may be married women now, and you have a kid hanging off your boob twenty hours a day, but that does not mean we're kept housewives. You need something to do, balance my books."

I had been thinking about it for a while, and now that I'd gotten the exclusive deal with LOFT, I needed more help on the business end of things. They'd sent me the paperwork and contracts, and I'd gone over them with a lawyer friend once Reese and I had gotten home from our honeymoon. I was starting next month representing the brand, and I was so fucking excited.

This deal meant the world to me. It would help take my blog and business to the next level. It would provide a real financial backing, and allow me to help contribute to my marriage. Not that Reese had been on my back, but I'd always promised myself to be independently financially secure if I was ever going to take that leap. He made more money than I did right now but, I was getting to his level with these deals.

"Seriously? You never wanted me involved in the blog or your business." Morgan looks kind of shocked.

"I know I didn't. I wanted to do everything on my own. But now that I have to file an LLC, and protect myself and file quarterly taxes and all of these other things I'm not sure how to do ... I need you."

Morgan considered me for a second, and then threw her poorly knitted blanket over the side of the couch. "I'm so in! Okay, so first we have to register you, and then set up a business bank account, get you on QuickBooks ..."

She rambled, speaking a language I didn't know half of. I was the beauty, she was the brains. Now my operation would be legitimate, and my sister could stop knitting and play with numbers and math, the two things she loved almost as much as Jeff and Carina.

My phone dings as she goes on.

Reese: *Be home in ten. Long day. I need my wife and a pint of ice cream and an Avengers movie marathon.*

I smiled, having already stocked the freezer with his favorite flavor knowing he was coming off of two night shifts in a row. For years, I'd worried about him as a best friend. And now, I still took care of him, but just on a deeper level. It was cosmic, and I wouldn't admit fate had a hand, but I would tell him from time to time that we were definitely made to find each other.

Erin: *Sounds perfect. I love you, carrots.*
  Reese: *I love you, peas.*

W e walked through an older section of Philadelphia, one that had once housed blue-collar families and was now being gentrified. I'd noticed at least two string band clubs that had buildings down here, and the old Philly vibe had me in a good mood.

"What's the restaurant we're going to?" We usually never came down to South Philly.

Reese looks over at me, his hand laced through mine. "This German place I heard was good. They're building this area back up, and this is a newer restaurant."

"Sounds good. As long as we don't have to eat Wiener schnitzel, because then I have a feeling you'll be making wiener jokes all night."

"It sounds like you'll be making wiener jokes." Reese raises an eyebrow at me.

He continues to lead me down a street, that looks residential instead of one with businesses and up and coming nightlife. "How much farther is this restaurant? These boots are pinching my toes."

The weather has turned cold in the two months since our

wedding. December in Philly is beautiful, bringing a whole new season of fashion, but it's freaking cold. I decided on black jeans, a black turtleneck, and maroon suede knee-high boots. The outfit was classy and sexy, and the boots were gorgeous. But they freaking hurt, and the heel was a little too high for the walk Reese was taking me on.

"You'll soon see, my bride." He bends down and kisses my cheek while we continue to walk.

I cringe. "Ugh, stop it. I told you I hate that. I love you, but I hate that nickname. Peas, baby, even sugar bear, I'd take. But my bride sounds creepy, like you're going to kidnap me or something."

Reese stops us in the middle of the street, this residential part of the city somewhat empty, and faces me toward him. "Maybe I am kidnapping you. But it's for a good reason. Turn around."

I turn around, looking at the brick front of a row home, one that looks the same as the others surrounding it, aside from the bright red front door.

"Um ... okay?" I don't get it.

"This could be ours." He looks at me, nervous and expectant.

"Um, husband, are you hiding a boatload of money I don't know about? Because you know that what's mine is yours now." I put a hand on my hip.

"No boatload of money, sorry. But ... I do own this place."

I turn to stare at him. "Okay, now I'm confused."

Reese walks us closer, and I see the C carved into one of the cement bricks the make up the stoop. "Well, I should say, my family owns this place. It was actually my great-grandparents home, back when everyone still grew up in the city. A couple of months ago, my parents were thinking about selling it. I asked them to save it for me, or if I could buy it."

"I didn't know your family owned a home down here." I peek over at him, surprised.

"So there are some things I've managed to keep hidden from you." He smirks.

I hit his bicep. "Hey, we're married now, you have to tell me all of your secrets."

Reese rolls his eyes. "I've told you every one of my secrets since I was seven. Except that I was in love with you. But I eventually told you."

I feel my neck heat when he says he's in love with me, and I still can't believe that I married my best friend. How weird is life?

"So you bought it a few months ago, eh? Pretty cocky of you to assume that you'd need it." I lean into him.

"I was so confident that you'd come around to make good on our pact. That's all. Want to go inside?" He's oddly quiet for him, and I nod yes.

Reese retrieves a key from his pocket, and steps in front of me to unlock the bright red door. We step inside and he flicks the hall light on.

"Now, it needs a lot of work. But ... I know how you love to design and create. So I thought you might enjoy that. We can pool our money and get a home renovation loan, since we won't have to pay a mortgage or rent." He walks us farther in. "There are three bedrooms and a basement, and this floor has your usual kitchen, living room, small laundry room and dining room, although we can knock all the walls out and make it an open concept, if you want."

I listen to him and the walls come to life, moving, shifting, ideas of colors and furniture forming. "I love it. Yes."

This is absolutely where we should be. History, so deep and rich, is running through this house. I'm a Collins now, and this meant a lot to Reese to have his parents keep it for us.

"The best part ... there is a finished attic. I thought maybe we could turn that into your office."

I walk to him, pulling his chin into my hands. "Have I told you lately how much I love you?"

He puts a finger to his chin. "Hmm, yes. But I'll always gladly hear it again.

"I love you. And this place. When can we start?" The DIY queen inside of me was itching to come out.

"Whenever you want. It's ours."

T wo things I love about my wife.

One, that she doesn't mind sleeping on a mattress on the floor.

Two, that she also doesn't mind eating cheesesteaks on a mattress on the floor. Half-naked ... that's another important point.

"This whole place smells like paint. I love it." Her eyes go wide as she bites into her sandwich, sighing as she swallows.

I tickle her leg. "You're insane. Who lives like this? And who enjoys it?"

"Me." She swells with pride.

It's been six months since we started work on the row home, and two weeks since we moved in. My lease on my apartment was up, which was the place we'd been living since we got married. Erin had given her apartment up long ago, so our only option was to move into our chaos and construction. We'd known about the deadline, but then Erin had insisted we needed to upgrade our master bathroom, and redo the floors on the second level, and so here we were, in the middle of sawdust and sink fixtures, eating our dinner and sleeping on the floor.

It was fun though, doing the renovation together. It was our first big project as a married couple, and we'd had our fair share of arguments over it already. But, we'd also had triumphs. The kitchen and living room were the first rooms we'd tackled, and they came out beautifully. As always, Erin's eye for design had been spot-on, and she'd really increased the value of our house, while making our humble abode a home.

"How was work? Did Preston say anything about Jill again?" My wife wipes a spot of cheese that dripped onto her chin.

"Work was okay. One of my babies, the little Asian boy, remember him? He'd been with us for six weeks and he finally got discharged, so that was nice to see. But right as I was getting off shift, they brought in a brand new baby who was born today, with a heart defect. It doesn't look good, from what I heard."

CHOP had been more rewarding than even I'd imagined. I was on life-saving cases, and I'd actually been able to stand in the room with the scrub nurses on some of the neonatal surgeries.

"And Preston said he's asking her tonight. He's a nervous wreck." I chuckled.

He wasn't asking Erin's friend to get married, just to move in. But for my friend, it was a huge step. He'd overcome a lot since we'd all gone on that double date, and I was happy for them.

We both eat the rest of our sandwiches, Erin scrolling through her phone some of the time and answering messages. Even though I'm not on social media, I don't mind that it's her life. I kind of like it that way, that I'm a little secret she pulls out sometimes for her followers.

"Oh, I'm so tired." She snuggles down into the pillows and comforter on our makeshift bed.

I've been thinking a lot since we started our renovation, about all this house will hold. And now that we've almost been married a year, I think I can say this without freaking her out.

Oh, who am I kidding? This is definitely going to freak her out. But that has never stopped me from doing anything when it comes to Erin.

"Let's have a baby." I scoot across the mattress on my side, snuggling up to her back and nuzzling in her hair.

"Is this going to be the same kind of negotiation we had when we had sex for the first time? Because this one is a little more involved. You have to pay an arm and a leg for this end result." She laces her fingers through mine and brings our joined hands up to rest just below her breasts.

"I'm serious. Think about a baby, cuter than Carina," I tease.

"No one is cuter than Carina," she scolds me, defending our godchild.

"Okay, you're right ... just as cute as Carina. Except with dark hair and dimples. And your monkey toes, and my crooked earlobes. We'll teach him or her all of the songs on the *Star Wars* soundtrack, and how to get the best deals when shopping online. Come on, you basically live with a raiser of tiny humans."

I grinned into her neck, hoping and praying that she says yes. I may be joking about our future child's qualities, but I wasn't joking about having a child. I wasn't a male NICU nurse for shits and giggles, I really loved babies. And kids. They said you loved your kid even if you didn't like other people's kids, and I did like other people's kids. So I would *really* love my own.

Erin flipped over, her hair flying through the air as she turned to face me. Her hands traced the stubble on my jaw, and her wedding and engagement rings caught the moonlight coming through the window behind our bed. *Our* bed ... it was still so surreal. Who knew that tricking your childhood best friend, and lifetime crush, into marrying you would actually work.

Her mocha-colored eyes glint with an idea. "I'll make you a

deal. If, by the time I'm thirty-three, we still don't have a baby, then I'll let you knock me up."

I smiled, holding out my right pinky for her to loop hers around. "It's a pact."

Erin hugged her pinky against mine, and we kissed. Pinky promises are a binding oath between us.

Too bad I'm going to do everything in my power to get her pregnant before then.

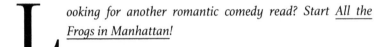

L ooking for another romantic comedy read? Start <u>All the Frogs in Manhattan</u>!

ALSO BY CARRIE AARONS

Do you want your **FREE** Carrie Aarons eBook?

All you have to do is **sign up for my newsletter**, and you'll immediately receive your free book!

Then, check out all of my books, available in Kindle Unlimited!

Standalones:

If Only in My Dreams

Foes & Cons

Love at First Fight

Nerdy Little Secret

That's the Way I Loved You

Fool Me Twice

Hometown Heartless

The Tenth Girl

You're the One I Don't Want

Privileged

Elite

Red Card

Down We'll Come, Baby

As Long As You Hate Me

On Thin Ice

All the Frogs in Manhattan

Save the Date

ABOUT THE AUTHOR

Author of romance novels such as Fool Me Twice and Love at First Fight, Carrie Aarons writes books that are just as swoon-worthy as they are sarcastic. A former journalist, she prefers the love stories of her imagination, and the athleisure dress code, much better.

When she isn't writing, Carrie is busy binging reality TV, having a love/hate relationship with cardio, and trying not to burn dinner. She lives in the suburbs of New Jersey with her husband, two children and ninety-pound rescue pup.

Please join her readers group, Carrie's Charmers, to get the latest on new books, exclusive excerpts and fun giveaways.

You can also find Carrie at these places:
Website
Amazon
Facebook
Instagram
TikTok
Goodreads